"Victory over sin through faith in the finished work of Jesus Christ is the modern church's most under-taught truth. In a book where C.S.Lewis's Narnia meets Oswald Chambers, God's provision for the abundant Christian life vibrantly comes alive in the Land of Charis."

-Jon Quast, New Tribes Mission

"The Well is a great book. It is a journey that leads the hungry-hearted believer to grace. Bisbee's adventure to Charis tells the story of progress in the life of the follower of Christ toward freedom. I was hungry and wondering if there was any life in Christianity? Is that your story? Then this book is for you!"

-Steve Williams, retired city worker

"The Well communicates a 'ground-breaking' concept that has been within our Bibles for centuries. This incredible book delivers such a thought-provoking story -- it provides well-grounded inspiration in our walk with the Lord. My fervent prayer is that many will read the contents and experience the life-altering change the message invokes."

-Trish Eachus-Crabtree, Author, Poet & Free-Lance Editor

"The Well: Journey to Charis is a novel that illustrates the true picture of God's grace with complex characters and a riveting plot. This allusion is purposed with extreme intentionality and detail. The reader can be certain that this novel incorporates the Judeo Bible not only through large concepts but also in character flaws, dialogue, and nuances. Reader: be in tune."

-Jenna Blyler and Brittany Jordan, college students

"What a fantastic book! I was captivated from the very beginning as I read about a journey to true freedom that so many in the church fail to embark upon. So many wonderful truths about God's grace and yet very entertaining as well. Everyone should read this book!"

-Pastor Mike Roddy, Ignite Church, St. Marys Ga

The Well

JOURNEY TO CHARIS

Mike Gaylor

WESTBOW
PRESS®
A DIVISION OF THOMAS NELSON
& ZONDERVAN

Scripture quotations are from The Holy Bible, English Standard Version®
(ESV®), copyright © 2001 by Crossway, a publishing ministry of
Good News Publishers. Used by permission. All rights reserved.

WestBow Press books may be ordered through booksellers or by contacting:

WestBow Press
A Division of Thomas Nelson & Zondervan
1663 Liberty Drive
Bloomington, IN 47403
www.westbowpress.com
1 (866) 928-1240

ISBN: 978-1-5127-4374-6 (sc)
ISBN: 978-1-5127-4375-3 (hc)
ISBN: 978-1-5127-4373-9 (e)

Library of Congress Control Number: 2016908521

Print information available on the last page.

WestBow Press rev. date: 06/07/2016

The Land of Charis

TABLE OF CONTENTS

I am deeply grateful to those who have helped me in bringing Bisbee's story to life. I wish to thank Jon Quast, Deb Metz, and Trish Eachus-Crabtree for their wisdom and guidance in the early stages of the work. I am thankful for the "team"; Susan Jordan, Brittany Jordan, and Jenna Blyler, who sacrificed countless hours in the editing process. Their contribution and patience were enormous. A special thanks to Jenna Blyler for the illustrations included within this book. Lastly, I wish to thank my wife Karen, not only for the sacrifice she made in giving me the time to write, but also for her valuable suggestions concerning Bisbee's story. She is my best friend.

○➤╫⬠•○•⬠╫◄○

I dedicate this book to my mother, Alice Smith Gaylor. Her love of reading, passion for observing nature, and our countless walks up "the hill" behind our house, helped to inspire this story.

CHAPTER 1

COOPERS CAVE

"Life started to unravel the day I fell into Coopers Cave..."

Gripping the worn arms of his leather chair, Bisbee braced for the impact that he knew was only moments away. His small-third story room was vulnerable to attack, and yet he refused to leave its familiar setting. If he was going to die, his chair was as good a place as any to end what had become to him a miserable existence. The anticipated collision was not long in coming: he was knocked to the floor and a small cut opened on his forehead. Bisbee's home was still intact but his nerves were unraveling like a tight spool of fishing line. Climbing back into his chair, Bisbee buried his tall frame deeper into the soft leather.

His heart was broken, crushed by the weight of a darkness he did not understand. Struggling to his feet, he pressed his face against the glass of a small wood-framed window and stared into the valley. The cry of a screech owl broke the silence of the night as it lifted its prey into the air. It had been another long, sleepless night.

A full moon cast shadows on the trees revealing a heavy mist rising from the earth. The sun would soon appear and with it, another day of doubt and fear. There had been a time when each new day brought excitement and adventure to Bisbee; however, those days had long passed, leaving him as but a nightly shadow, dimming with the morn.

Tears ran down his cheeks, and dripped into the cold cup of tea that he held tightly to his chest. Something was terribly wrong. Bisbee recognized a foreboding *darkness that dwelled inexplicably in his soul, gripping him in its embrace of despair.*

Turning from the window, he peered into the blackness of his small sitting room. His loft had become a hiding place, sheltering him from the world he now feared. Here, he could be alone with his thoughts, alone with his misery.

Sitting back down in his soft leather chair, Bisbee closed his eyes, took a sip of salty tea, and traveled back in his mind to the day he first met Marnin. How wonderful it was for Bisbee to recall their friendship, to bathe in the special bond that they shared. Marnin was dearer to his soul than life itself. In the midst of his present distress, the memory felt pleasant, calming Bisbee's quaking heart.

The day he met Marnin was an ordinary day not unlike a thousand preceding it. Bisbee was walking down the dirt road leading to Dunkirk, whistling a happy tune, when he passed by Sanford Ledge. Looking up, he saw a man sitting on the edge of a huge rock, gazing into the distance; Bisbee would have passed by but the stranger was intriguing. Calling out to the man, Bisbee asked him what he was looking at. Marnin gently replied, "Come and see."

Reluctantly, Bisbee accepted his invitation. Climbing a steep rocky trail, which circled back around to the ledge, he sat down next to the man, allowing his feet to hang off the edge. The next few hours passed as if they were only moments in time. Bisbee was so fascinated by the mysterious man that he returned the next day and everyday thereafter.

Continuing to reflect on the memory of it all, two things impressed Bisbee about Marnin. He was amazed at how much his new friend already knew about him... and then there was his voice. When Marnin spoke, it was like a soft spring rain falling on the desert sand, soaking the ground to awaken seeds buried deep in deadness. Bisbee slowly became aware that he had been living life for all of the wrong reasons. He realized that life without his new friend had not been worth living.

Bisbee's entire way of looking at things changed as a result of the time he spent with Marnin. He would never forget the day that he decided to follow his new friend. What started as a friendship became so much more. As a token of their bond, Marnin gave Bisbee a copy of a map and writings, which at first confused him. Marnin promised that in time he would understand them more and more. Bisbee had become captivated by the love of the one whom he would come to know as the Master.

An old crow landed in a nearby pine tree. Its incessant cries jarred Bisbee's attention back to the valley below. With every scream of the crow, another Beast was released into Harness, causing misery and destruction. In an effort to block the terror of this nightly reality, he allowed his mind to drift back to a happier time.

Bisbee recalled the day he decided to move his growing family to the land of Harness. His decision to relocate was the culmination of months of struggle and heated debate with his bride of eighteen years. Avonlea had heard stories of the Beasts of Harness, which Bisbee counted as nothing more than folklore. The last thing she wanted was to subject their two children to danger. Stephen was on the verge of puberty and Lorelai was just starting first grade. She admitted that living in Dunkirk was becoming unbearable due to the anger the village people possessed toward Marnin; yet, she did not warm to the idea of living among Beasts.

She never understood why the people of Dunkirk hated Marnin, but it seemed to involve a long-ago dispute over a grove of trees, which happened long ago. Locking horns in an epic battle of wills, Bisbee finally wore her down. Although Avonlea understood why they could no longer live in Dunkirk, she was not convinced Harness was their best option.

The land of Harness did provide a more structured and peaceful existence in accordance with all Marnin taught. At least that is what was written in the information packets that arrived weekly at their doorstep. Pictures of rolling green hills and crops growing in the field gave no hint of the presence of anything evil or destructive.

When Bisbee asked Marnin about Harness, he was strangely silent. The Master would simply smile and change the subject. Inwardly irritated by Marnin's hesitation to give him counsel, Bisbee stopped bringing it up and began packing. He refused to allow tales of mythical creatures to guide his life.

It was not long after arriving in Harness, during an evening stroll with Avonlea, that the couple encountered the Beasts. Turning the corner at Slater Crossing they were struck by a presence, which carried with it an odor they had never smelled before.

As Bisbee stepped in front of Avonlea to protect her, they both braced for an ambush that never came. A pleasant evening stroll had quickly turned into a terrifying nightmare. Mere shadows in the darkness had left them with the distinct impression of terror.

Living in Harness soon became miserable as a result of the presence of these Beasts. Avonlea had been right, as usual. Bisbee was reminded anew why he had chosen her. To her credit she resisted pointing out the obvious fact that he had made a poor decision. Displaying a leathery toughness, Avonlea went about making the best of life in this new land.

Marnin never abandoned Bisbee while in Harness. His meetings with the Master, which were never planned and yet always appreciated, encouraged him. They would spend entire afternoons walking along lazy streams or climbing one of the many hills of Harness. When Bisbee would invite Marnin to stay for dinner, the Master usually had something more pressing. Although Bisbee never asked, Marnin seemed uncomfortable spending too much time in Harness.

As the years pressed on, the Beasts grew in size and number. Bisbee's numerous attempts to discuss these creatures with his neighbors and friends proved futile. There seemed to be a code of silence concerning the Beasts. Met with blank stares and shallow responses, he finally gave up trying to engage his fellow Harnessites in discussing their common misery. Even though Bisbee was frustrated by their silence, he refused to accept what all of Harness had come to believe: the Beasts were an unavoidable part of life.

Bisbee instead decided to battle the Beasts himself, using different methods and strategies, but in time, failure and exhaustion took its toll. The inevitable results of fighting the foe left him hopeless. One night, overwhelmed by the thought of living among such creatures, he ventured out against Avonlea's pleadings. Bisbee grabbed the weapons he had left by the back door and headed out into the darkness. Armed and ready to end the Beasts' reign of terror, he quietly crept deeper and deeper into the black forest. Following his pounding heart rather than his thinking mind, Bisbee walked all night long through Harness. Not only was he unsuccessful, Bisbee had trouble even finding one of the Beasts.

A familiar sound brought Bisbee back to the reality of his leather chair and his cup of cold tea. The crow had screamed again, five, now six times; it was a busy night for the destroyers. Feelings of hopelessness flooded him. He hated crows. He hated the Beasts, but most of all he hated the thought that he had brought his family to such a place.

Bisbee picked up a stack of letters sitting on the table next to him. They were written on green stationery and had been delivered to him by his friend, Mitch Miller. The letters were filled with descriptions of a land called Charis. Mitch had refused to reveal the origin of the correspondence, only that he had found them on his doorstep. Bisbee's name was on the envelope with a stamp marked, "URGENT." Having no clue as to why they were sent specifically to him, Bisbee had received the letters only because a trusted friend had delivered them.

He had pored over the writings for weeks, until they became crumpled and torn. A dozen times he had tossed them in the trashcan, only to dig them out again. At one point he had even hidden the green letters under the floorboards of his den in order to keep them from Avonlea. Any hint that he believed there to be a land better than the one she presently endured, was sure to begin another argument.

The letters told of a fount called the Well of Chayah that had been discovered in a land called Charis. The Well was described as a place of death, as well as a source of life. Captivated by this apparent anomaly, Bisbee could not stop thinking about it. How could a single Well yield both death and life? Unable to understand the writings, they had become just one more source of frustration.

Bisbee had contemplated a journey to Charis, but knowing it would anger the Elders, he soon abandoned the idea. Besides, to exchange the predictability of life in Harness for the uncertainty of Charis was a risky proposition.

If Harness was nothing else, it was certainly a place of routine. Year by year it produced similar results. Operating like a huge machine: whatever was planted was harvested. What the Elders planned, came to pass. The leadership of Harness controlled all aspects of life and labor.

The Elders implied that to question their authority was to challenge Marnin himself, although Marnin seemed to have little to do with the operation of it all. The Elders appeared to be content with the external appearance of submission with little care for internal matters. The heart could boil with anger as long as the lips curled upwards and the eyes danced a happy jig.

There were not a lot of surprises in Harness. The Land seemed to exist on calculated outcomes. No one stepped out of line or questioned how things were, they just were. The Elders made sure a sense of shame followed those who dragged their feet in Harness.

Living in Harness brought Bisbee an external sense of comfort and security, but at what cost? The Beasts still roamed the land, waiting for the sun to set and the entire land lived in a culture of fear.

Bisbee climbed the ranks in Harness quickly. Given job after job, he excelled with ease at whatever the Elders asked him to do. The busyness of his labor numbed Bisbee. The positions of authority he received fed his ego, and yet he knew something was missing. The Beasts still ruled the night, which made any activity during the day seem ridiculously phony. Tempted to pull away from his duties in Harness, Bisbee, for some unknown reason resisted, choosing to continue the charade.

As the nightly attacks increased, Harness adopted a mentality of survival. Each morning the damage that the Beasts had brought was dealt with in a systematic and calculated way. Ruined buildings and trampled crops were cleaned up and life went on as usual. Farmers planted and replanted in the hope that their crops would be spared, if but for a season. Stores were boarded up to limit the destruction.

At the weekly Meeting Place, a feeble attempt was made by the Elders to confront the nightly terror. Training was offered on how to counter the attacks, but when the Beasts came, all the instruction was useless to stop the rampage. The people of Harness hunkered down each night and hoped for the best. Any suggestion that the "Destructive Ones" could be ultimately conquered was met with resistance and ridicule by the fearful counsel of the Elders. It slowly occurred to Bisbee that something more was needed than another strategy or plan that the Elders offered.

Bisbee decided to read the letters once more and found he was longing for this land of peace and freedom. Unlike Harness, the Land of Charis promised victory over these Beasts. Could it be true that there was there such a Well? Did a land of true victory even exist?

Placing the letters back on the table, he recalled many warning signs he had seen posted in Harness depicting Charis as a land to be avoided. The signs were barely readable, having suffered both time and neglect. The harbingers were unneeded, as the Elders had diligently labored to etch in the peoples' minds a fear of traveling to this far away land. They hated the topic of Charis, and when it surfaced, the Elders attacked it with veracious verbosity.

Why would the letters point him to a land that the Elders of Harness had warned against? He had heard others speak of Charis, but most dismissed it as a journey either unnecessary or not worth the risks. Few ever returned to tell of the adventure and when they did, their reports were quickly denounced.

Wild rumors abounded concerning the effect on those who journeyed to Charis. The Elders portrayed the land as being inhabited with demons and it was even described as a place of death. Placing the green letters back on the table, Bisbee sunk deeper into his chair.

Traveling back further, he recalled the day he had fallen into Coopers Cave. Bisbee had been returning from a morning spent with Marnin, when he came across fresh footprints from one of the Beasts. A smoldering pile of dung near an opening in Aker's Hill drew him to the cave. While lowering himself down through the narrow entrance, the root that Bisbee had been holding onto suddenly cracked. Unable to stop his fall, he crashed into a pile of rocks on the floor of the cave. Reaching for his light, Bisbee came face to face with a scene that would haunt him thereafter. Etched in the granite wall of the cave was a clear warning of epic proportion. Terrified by the pronouncement of a coming disaster, targeting the people of Harness, Bisbee emerged from the cave, shaken to his core. The writings on the wall had indicated an unknown disease would soon spread throughout Harness, decimating the populace.

He immediately returned and began desperately searching for the green letters that Mitch had delivered.

Bisbee became hungry for answers, panic-stricken to discover the source of the sickness predicted in Coopers Cave. Were the Beasts a part of the plague that would come?

Loud bellowing from the nightscape filled his tiny room as Bisbee dug his fingernails into the leather chair. Terrified by the incessant blasts, he crawled deeper under his worn quilt, and plugged his ears. The night air was filled with misery and torments. The Beasts were becoming more aggressive and Bisbee seemed to be the only one who understood the urgency of the situation. He knew the journey to Charis was their only hope.

CHAPTER 2

THE JOURNEY NORTH

And so, one autumn morning, Bisbee bid farewell to Avonlea and headed north through the narrow streets of Harness. Passing Miller's bakery, he happily waved to his old friend Mitch. His childhood buddy had almost died from a heart attack earlier in the year. It had been a difficult road to recovery. Covered with flour from head to toe, he appeared ghostly through the thick window. The smile on Mitch's face told Bisbee word had gotten out about his journey to Charis. His son Stephen, (who had always struggled keeping secrets), had most likely told him.

Bisbee thought about his decision to conceal his trip from the Elders. The only one on the counsel that had appeared sympathetic was an Elder named Tourgen. Bisbee had seen in his eyes a desire to reach out, to speak to Bisbee concerning the Beasts, but Tourgen's fear of the counsel had held him back.

Pausing at the outskirts of town, he sat down on a small stonewall. Bisbee carefully unfolded the map that he had received from Marnin, along with the writings. Their contents had become a constant source of light and encouragement. Marnin had expressed his sadness to Bisbee that not all his followers had given the map and his writings the attention that they deserved. Bisbee had determined never to neglect them.

He carefully folded the documents and placed them back in his worn leather satchel. Bisbee then checked his supplies and made sure the green letters were still there. Leaning back against a stump, he closed his eyes and thought about the journey ahead.

How had he overlooked the numerous landmarks on the map pointing to the Land of Charis? How foolish he had been to regard the warning signs in Harness as of greater importance than the map and writings Marnin had given him. Men had posted the signs, not Marnin. Marnin had given him the map, not man. Why had it taken him so long to discover the emptiness of Harness? Bisbee was thankful he had become desperate for answers. He was grateful to whomever had sent him the green letters.

After taking a final look back at the sleepy village, Bisbee turned and walked away from the life he had grown accustomed to in Harness. Embarking on an adventure filled with uncertainty, the man who had nothing left to lose, slowly turned toward the forest. In that defining moment, as the last few shadows of the night were being hunted by the rising sun, Bisbee became The Traveler.

Passing by Sanford Ledge, Bisbee smiled as he remembered the hours he had spent there with Marnin. Those days, so long ago, seemed beautifully simplistic. His focus was all about him and the Master, sharing life together. Longing for those days to return, Bisbee wondered if life could ever be simple again.

Tempted to stop off in Dunkirk to visit old friends, Bisbee resisted. He forced himself to remain on the trail as he passed by his old neighborhood. Whatever it was that drew a man to his past, pulled hard on his soul. What a useless endeavor it would be to rummage about the old haunts. Bisbee concluded that every bit of energy must be reserved for the adventure ahead.

The sun was sinking in the horizon when he reached the path leading into North Woods. Walking past a majestic elm tree, he paused long enough to see his reflection in a quiet pond that bordered the forest. Staring into the placid waters, Bisbee thought about his life and the kind of man he had become.

The years had been good to him. A gentle aging process had allowed him to keep most of his hair, and the lines on his face were barely noticeable. Tall and awkward, he laughed as he looked down at his feet. As long as he could remember they had been oversized and a source of constant teasing. His brown curly hair had begun to whiten and he was missing a tooth, which was barely noticeable since it was far back in his mouth. He walked with a slight limp, caused by his fall into Coopers Cave. Bisbee did not consider himself handsome, but Avonlea loved him and what else could he ask for?

Bisbee's friends knew him as a quiet, reflective man, who was well liked by most. He was a man who was able to mind his own business and remain calm in difficult situations. Occasionally, Bisbee would come alive at a gathering of friends, but he had to feel at ease in order to let his guard down. His fear of being ridiculed for something he either said or did brought back painful memories from his childhood. Being the youngest in a big family had its downside. For good, for bad, Bisbee was himself, and he had become comfortable in his own skin.

Bisbee had met his future bride during the annual square dance at the Dunkirk Fairgrounds. Having watched the beautiful stranger for most of the night, he found it increasingly difficult to take his eyes off of her. Finally, not being able to stand it any longer, Avonlea walked across the floor and introduced herself. A silent, awkward moment ensued, until she finally broke into a wide grin. Speaking loud enough for all to hear, she asked him if he was just going to stare at her all night or was he going to ask her to dance. She then locked her arm in his and pulled him onto the dance floor. His clumsiness was apparent to all that night, but Avonlea simply laughed and whispered in his ear, "Who cares." Somewhere in the midst of their fourth do-si-do, he had already fallen in love.

Bisbee smiled at the memory of her boldness. He loved her sassiness. Avonlea's fiery temper and sharp tongue had gotten him in trouble with the Elders on a number of occasions. He had fussed with her about speaking to the Elders in such sharp tones, but secretly wished he could be as bold.

Moving on from the pond, he walked down a rocky trail and was instantly swallowed by a tall pine canopy of evergreens. Slender wooden soldiers, they served as "guardians of the way" to the Land of Charis. The trail took Bisbee due north through the Wilderness of Yabesh, which bordered Harness for as far as anyone cared to travel.

The journey soon turned into the same daily regiment. The long days of hiking were followed by lonely nights in a tent. From the shelter of his canvas cave and with the light of a single candle, Bisbee found great encouragement as he poured over Marnin's writings. Along with that precious parchment, the green letters that Mitch had delivered to him were beginning to make sense.

Bisbee was happy to finally discover the Stream of Naphash. He had journeyed for weeks through a low country called Otser, which was a dry and dusty land, filled with a foreboding sense of nothingness. From his childhood, Bisbee had heard tales of a tribe of warriors who roamed this low country. Stories of great exploits, in a certain forest north of Otser, had been told in the ears of children for generations. It was believed that this tribe entered the low country in search of young men who were hungry for battle. He was relieved he had seen no sight of them.

As he stood in the midst of the Stream of Naphash, the fast moving, cool water flowed over his weary feet and cheered his heart. According to the Map, this creek would eventually lead him to the small village of Kobel Town, which bordered the Land of Charis.

Following the stream north, the trail became steep, and the journey became increasingly difficult. Then one evening, as he was setting up his tent, the Traveler heard a familiar voice.

"Bisbee, my boy."

Startled, he saw Marnin sitting like a king on a huge rock, overlooking the trail. It was good to hear his voice. Like music to his ears, Marnin spoke with clear, resonating tones, reassuring Bisbee's troubled spirit.

Pleasantly locked in the moment, all Bisbee could do was stare at Marnin. The Master was beautiful to look upon. His long flowing white hair danced in the breeze, and his emerald green eyes seemed to change shades as he turned his head from side to side. Marnin's brown, weathered face glowed with happiness. The sight of the Master sitting on the rock, reminded him of the days when they sat together on Sanford Ledge. Their times together always had a soothing effect on Bisbee. Marnin was close like a best friend; yet, their relationship was beginning to take on a complexity that the Traveler did not understand.

As Marnin gathered wood for the fire, Bisbee continued to pitch camp.

By the glow of the campfire, they unfolded the map that Bisbee had been carrying. Harness was southeast of their present location. The Master then reached into his satchel and pulled out a second map that Bisbee had never seen before. Old and leathery, the map intrigued Bisbee. Marnin finally looked up.

"The answer you seek is in Charis, Bisbee, but there are many dangers."

"Is that a map of Charis?" asked Bisbee.

Marnin nodded. "It's time you see the Land with, shall we say, more clarity."

He unfolded the ancient map, spreading it out before the fire. With great care and precision, the Master walked Bisbee through each step in Charis, until he was satisfied that his friend could close his eyes and still visualize it.

"Ascending Hill is your first test. At first glance, it appears as if it is nothing more than a hill to walk down, but it holds a very important lesson. Everything you learn, Bisbee, at each juncture, is vital to your understanding of Charis."

"You'll be going with me, right?"

"No, not at first but I'll send you a guide."

"How will I know him when I see him?" asked Bisbee.

Marnin smiled, "Trust me, you'll know him."

Sitting together in silence, they stared into the glowing embers. Bisbee's mind trailed off, and he found himself internally staring at the etching he had seen on the cave wall. Coopers Cave had left a hot seal of painful remembrance deep within Bisbee's soul. Since that traumatic evening, nightmares terrorized his subconscious to the point of cold-sweated desperation. He longed to share this experience with Marnin: he needed comfort and he needed counsel. Bisbee looked up to see the reflection of the fire dancing off Marnin's face. He could stand the wait no longer. In a moment of unguarded trust, Bisbee spoke out.

"Who was the dark creature in the cave?"

His heart had spoken before his mind could object. Still staring into the fire, a look of concern spread across Marnin's face.

"You saw something in a cave?"

"Yes, something or someone."

Bisbee fell silent. Flashes of the memory began moving across his mind. Climbing out of Coopers Cave, the moon had suddenly appeared from behind the clouds. Light broke into the entrance, revealing the creature hiding in the rocks. As much as he tried to forget what he saw, the image haunted him. Determined to keep the nightmare from the Master, Bisbee finally spoke, "It was nothing."

Marnin leaned forward, "Go ahead, tell me."

Bisbee spoke softly, "I only saw it for a moment. It had a twisted, warped head, and its skin was pale. Its eyes were the color of blood, not a normal red; it was a dark, sickly shade. It let out a low gurgling sound, as if were drowning in its own mucus, and then it just slithered off into the darkness."

Bisbee was surprised at his ability to recall so many details. The memory sickened him, as it had many times before.

Marnin stared into the fire.

"He works for the enemy."

Deeply disturbed to hear of an enemy perhaps more hideous than the creature in the cave, Bisbee became light headed. How strong was this foe, and was this nameless adversary pursuing him? The revelation was disheartening, and yet, it would answer so many questions. Were there invisible forces at work in Harness? Was this enemy the wellspring of the misery and fear that Bisbee had come to know? Was it responsible for the Beasts?

Marnin waited patiently for Bisbee to process the shocking truth of an enemy. Looking intently into his eyes, the Master continued.

"As terrifying as the creature was to look upon, it has no power over you."

"Does it have a name?" Bisbee asked.

"It does, but you have no need to know it. The only name you need to remember is mine."

By launching this razor sharp arrow of truth, the Master held a quiet hope that his declaration would penetrate Bisbee's heart, relieving him of his fear of the enemy. To his disappointment, Bisbee deflected it from its intended mark. Marnin turned away, staring into the fire. Bisbee continued to press for more information with the same intense anxiety.

"Are the writings on the cave wall true?"

"Yes."

"Then I don't have much time, do I?"

"No. Bisbee, you need to know that the plague you read about in the cave has struck before, in fact, several times in different places. What will happen in Harness is a result of forces you do not understand. Your journey to Charis will not prevent the devastation that will certainly come upon Harness. Unfortunately, only a few will survive. The name of the plague is Sardis."

Bisbee swallowed so hard it made his eyes water. He thought of Avonlea and his children. Stephen was grown with a family of his own, and Lorelai was just turning eighteen. They had their lives ahead of them, or so he hoped. Would he ever see them again? Fully engulfed in shock, and yet partially relieved to know the truth, Bisbee struggled to digest Marnin's calm pronouncement of doom. He decided he would ask no further questions.

As Marnin rose to tend to the fire, Bisbee looked off into the darkness of the woods that now entombed him. He longed to draw closer to the fire with the Master, but the reality of an enemy lurking behind the trees of the night forest enslaved him with despair. Somewhere in the night, while internally wrestling with an invisible foe, Bisbee fell into a deep sleep and when he awoke... Marnin was gone.

As the sun began to rise over the Adina Mountains, Bisbee realized he was nearing his destination. Karmel Valley, in all its beauty, opened up before him at a turn in the road near Groman's Nose. Spring had come to the valley, and the fresh cut hay drying in the field reminded Bisbee of home. He had hoped he would see Marnin, but there was no sign of him now.

Crossing over a small stream, he climbed a grassy knoll. Tempted to stop and rest, Bisbee decided to press on, desiring to reach his destination by nightfall. He paused just long enough to study the map and then continued on his journey.

As the sun was setting, Bisbee discovered Nichols Hallow. A small trail led out of the tiny community that would guide Bisbee to Kobel Town. Bisbee decided to get a fresh start in the morning and set up camp under a rocky overhang.

As the morning broke, Bisbee found himself renewed in his passion to discover Charis. After eating a humble breakfast of cherry granola, Bisbee packed his supplies and headed down the trail leading north. He had passed several important landmarks when he found that the trail was becoming more and more overgrown. He soon became tangled in the overgrowth and fell in the thicket. Covered in dew, Bisbee smiled, his large feet had gotten in his way again.

Sitting in a tangled patch of Bishop's Goutweed, he looked to his left and saw a small opening in the bushes, which revealed the activity of a small town. In the very moment he stood up to brush himself off, an excited red robin flew past him. Pausing to perch on a nearby branch, she welcomed him to Kobel Town.

Red Robin

Turning off the trail, Bisbee walked down a stone embankment and entered the village.

Bisbee attempted to greet the locals, but the effort proved futile. Blank hollow faces deflected his happy smile as he entered the town. Boarded up shops and overgrown shrubbery lined the streets. There were no children playing in the sandlots, no happy chatter in the park. Abandoned churches had been converted to food kitchens for the poor. A dark shadow had descended on this little town, tucked away in the middle of nowhere: something was wrong.

Passing through a vacant neighborhood on the north end of town, Bisbee made a sharp right and entered the village cemetery. Large, bushy evergreens dotted the graveyard of cold marble slabs. Stone monuments, erected to remember the dead, silently stared at him. Green with moss and broken down with age and neglect, they reminded Bisbee that few ever remember the dead…

Pressing up the gentle slope, he carefully avoided stepping on the graves, weaving in and out between the granite markers. Pausing midway up the hill, Bisbee turned to face the village. The leaves of the maples and elms were budding, and the fresh leaves danced among the rooftops. Rusty church steeples dotted the township. Most had fallen, due to neglect, causing him to wonder if Marnin had forgotten this town. Perhaps the people had forgotten Marnin. The silent grey cemetery spoke of lives once lived, as the empty churches echoed their cry.

Could it be that Sardis had come to this town? Could the condition of this village be the results of the plague? The town had an appearance of life, but something hollow and eerie walked the streets. Its inhabitants moved as dry, dusty corpses, fulfilling the duties of daily living with no purpose beyond the sedentary moment.

A cold wind caught Bisbee unexpectedly, and he fought to catch his breath. Zipping his jacket, he continued up the hill. Excitement began surging through him as he climbed over a barbed wire fence dividing the plateau of death from the hay fields of Ascending Hill. The map had perfectly described the topography. A dozen steps took him to the crest which overlooked the Land of Charis. The sky was blue, a brighter blue than he had ever seen.

As he sat down in the soft alfalfa, Bisbee sensed the presence of the Master. He turned just in time to see Marnin coming out of a wooded area which lay next to the hay fields. It had been weeks since they had shared the warmth of the campfire together. Without speaking a word, he sat down next to Bisbee, and after exchanging a smile, they both looked into the valley.

The Land of Charis was smaller than Bisbee had expected. The valley spreading out before him was no wider than a mile and perhaps three miles long.

At the bottom of the hill he saw Living Stream flowing from a mountain spring, hidden in distant mountains. Meandering its way toward Kobel Town, it ran under Crossing Bridge at the spot of the Great Willow. On the other side of the Bridge, a grassy road climbed with a slight uphill grade toward an aged, majestic red barn. It was just as Marnin had described. Its simple rusty tin roof shone in the afternoon sun, as the door of the barn swung open and a group of women emerged laughing. They seemed to be carefree and full of happiness.

To the right of the barn was a hay field, ripe for the harvest. Bisbee spotted men thrashing the silage with long, sharp sickles. Rather than being exhausted by their labors, they talked, enjoying each others' company. Occasionally they threw their tools down for a friendly wrestling match in the soft clover.

Just beyond the barn was a large white farmhouse with a soft green lawn. Bisbee spotted rhubarb growing under the porch of the house and a wasp's nest the size of a small boulder hanging above a clothesline. Children ran and played in the shadow of the porch. A ceramic pitcher sat on a round white table by a door leading into a cellar, and glasses surrounded the pitcher, filled with a green foamy drink.

"Apple spice tea, there's no drink like it."

Bisbee got the feeling Marnin was about to launch down the hill in full stride after the beverage, but he remained next to him on the hill.

Beyond the house and across a low-lying ditch lay a densely wooded forest, which appeared to spread as far as the eye could see.

Bisbee spotted an old well on the left side of the porch. Green with overgrown vines and neatly tucked away under a lilac bush, it could barely be seen.

"Are you ready, my friend?" asked Marnin.

Bisbee would have never been so bold as to call the Master friend, but Marnin seemed to enjoy using the phrase.

"Yes, I'm ready," Bisbee replied.

Marnin smiled. "Yes, I think you are. Remember, Crossing Bridge is the only way into the Land of Charis, and you only enter one time. Once you are in Charis, Charis is in you. You may cross over the boundaries as many times as you wish, but you will never feel at home beyond its borders."

"Are you coming with me?"

"No." Marnin paused.

"There is something I need to warn you about, Bisbee. Although the Land of Charis holds the answer you have been seeking, you will face death in the midst of it."

Blood rushed out of Bisbee's face as he stared into the clover. He had read about death in the writings, but the thought of it always echoed distantly with a hollow ring. How could death be in a land marked out for life? Bisbee's chest had physically fallen, and sweat had broken out on his forehead. Marnin placed his hand on the Traveler's shoulder and spoke with a calm and steady voice. It was the same voice Bisbee had come to know and love.

"Don't be afraid. Sometimes we must drink death and life out of the same cup."

After a moment of contemplation, he looked back toward the valley. Confident of the Master's love, Bisbee reminded himself he could face anything. Marnin had not led him astray thus far. Tucking the map and the writings under his arm, the Traveler took his first steps toward Crossing Bridge.

Welcome to an adventure that only begins when you realize the journey is over. It is not a journey of the feet or of the mind, but one of faith. It is important to note that faith must be grounded in truth. The Bible will be our guide for the excursion ahead. Only by carefully following God's Word, can we confidently know that we are treading a path that will be as solid as granite under our feet. This book you hold in your hands is a declaration of our emancipation from sin, but be assured of this, it is not built on a balloon filled with the hot air of empty promises. The truth that this book declares will set you free from the tyranny of sin.

Perhaps you have heard the old expression; "There's an elephant in the room." It means there is a topic that needs discussing, and yet, everyone chooses to ignore it. Although most avoid the elephant topics, those are the very subjects that need to be addressed.

The "elephant" at large in the church today, is the self-life of the believer, and this propensity displays itself in the sinful behavior of the followers of Christ. Unable to ultimately conquer this "elephant," the church either ignores the beast or offers solutions that fall short of their intended goal. Within believers, the steamy dunghill of sin is addressed in distant theory rather than shoveled personally.

The Bible calls this "elephant" the flesh, and it grips us in a perpetual state of bondage. According to the Apostle Paul, this condition of servitude to sin was never meant to be the ongoing experience of the believer.[1]

Freedom from this slavery to sin is exactly what Jesus promised us if we continue to follow Him.[2] Since we know His promise is true then why are so few experiencing this freedom? Perhaps many have chosen to follow the teachings of men rather than Christ. There are those who attempt to lead us toward higher ground with empty platitudes and hollow drumbeats. They offer alternative routes to freedom; however, they all arrive at the same dead street of defeat.

As pastors, we bear a great responsibility to those who sit under our teaching. I challenge you; if you are a fellow pastor, to ask yourself the hard questions. Is the content of what you preach setting people free from the power of sin or is it sinking them deeper into the struggle? Are you experiencing true growth and freedom in Christ? Are you confident in the path you are treading spiritually?

I know firsthand the torment of passing under promising rain clouds only to end up dry and in bondage. I am weary of books filled with experiences, opinions and positivity, which at best, provide momentary cheer but do not provide the key to unlock the prison.

There is a clear path to victory, and it can only be in found in the Bible. Jesus offers us an abundant, overflowing life, and it does not include bondage.

Much of what you are about to read will be difficult to swallow. I have made no attempt to sheath the two-edged sword of scripture.[3] If you are hungry for truth, you will push the blade in deeper. The writer of Hebrews stated, "Strong meat belongs to those who are of full age."[4] Unlike the long list of books you may have tossed in the corner, I believe this book will point you to the truth of scripture. Simply stated, "There's meat on these bones."

The gateway leading into this amazing adventure defies logic. Even though it is available to all, there are very few who ever find it.[5] Like most adventures, this path is not without hardship and sacrifice. Along the journey you will need to discard many things you have been taught. Many things that have been written on the chalkboard of your mind will need to be erased. With every falsehood you toss on the trail, your backpack will get lighter and lighter. The sacred cows of religious practices will need to be slaughtered. The countless edicts of men will need to be burned.

Although the journey has a difficult beginning, once the destination is reached, life begins to make sense. Like a plant responds to sunlight, soil and water, you will begin to grow naturally, and the ease of it will amaze you. Paul warned us not to allow anyone to move us away from the simplicity of Christ.[6]

In stark contrast to the crushing weight of the constant pressing thumb of religion, the abundant life of Christ is light, carefree, and naturally spontaneous. Men complicate Christianity when they attempt to add human effort to the finished work of Christ. Paul did not teach "Christ and me," he declared, "Christ in me."[7]

There is no greater gift than knowledge. To wander in the darkness of uncertainty is to bump into a thousand walls of frustration and defeat. Conversely, to know the truth, in any area, is to walk in confidence, deflecting our lives from needless preoccupations and pointless endeavors.

Have you ever put a puzzle together and then toward the end of the project, realized that a few of the pieces were missing? Think of this book as a flashlight to help you find the last few pieces of the puzzle. The "picture" of true Christianity will come into glorious view, once the last few pieces of the puzzle are snapped in place. You will experience the Christian life from a whole new perspective.

This book is about a journey that will lead you to a fuller understanding and experience of all that you already possess in Christ. Christianity is a finished work, and the essence of our walk with Christ is a matter of receiving, not doing. All that we need for victory, we already possessed at the beginning of our walk with Christ. As a result, this book does not contain a list of things to "do," in order to grow.

When Jesus appeared on the shores of Galilee after His resurrection, He found the disciples in their boats, hard at work and yet empty, lonely and without fish.[8] He stood on the solid ground of the shore of Galilee, as they floated on unstable waters of the lake. Calling to them from the shore, He asked if they had any food. Staring into their empty nets, they were hungry and speechless. They learned that day a life apart from their Master yields nothing. Jesus commanded the disciples to cast their nets on the right side of the boat and when they did, the catch was overflowing. However, once on shore, they found Jesus had already prepared breakfast. None of the fish they had caught would be part of the meal.

As a new day dawned over the Sea of Galilee, Jesus invited them to "Come and dine."[9] Sound too easy? Busy cleaning fish? Maybe you've launched back out to do some more fishing because you thought it was the spiritual thing to do. When Jesus invites you to come and dine, the most spiritual thing that you can do is: well, "come and dine." Everything had been prepared beforehand, and all they had to do was to lay down their nets, stop their activity, and receive the meal that Jesus offered. There is nothing more natural than eating a meal.

Are you ready to simply "come and dine?" Like the old hymn says, "you may feast at Jesus' table all the time."[10] Don't hesitate; the fish are still hot.

CHAPTER 3

ASCENDING HILL

With every step down the hill, the Master's last words rang in Bisbee's ears. "You will face death in the land."

As he looked out over the valley, he saw nothing suggesting such a thing. Still, he could think of nothing else.

Why would death be present in Charis? Perhaps Marnin did not mean it literally. A symbolic death would be more acceptable to Bisbee's way of thinking than the traditional, permanent type. Perhaps the death of which Marnin spoke was a ceremony or ritual of some sort. The experience of death, in whatever shape or form, was something Bisbee desperately wanted to avoid.

Large, puffy clouds floated softly overhead. Prepared for a day of fishing, an eagle soared under the force of a strong east wind as it passed above Bisbee. At the bottom of the hill flowed Living Stream, babbling between its clay banks.

As Bisbee wrestled with Marnin's mysterious pronouncement of death, it occurred to the Traveler that everything he had just seen was a mystery. He had no idea how these forces of nature worked. How did the clouds float or the eagle soar? Where was the fountainhead of the stream and why did its source not dry up?

These mysteries were all inexplicable to Bisbee, and yet they were real. The concept of matter mixed perfectly with riddle to create reality. It dominated his thoughts. The death Marnin mentioned was certainly an enigma to Bisbee; yet, why could it not be as real as the clouds or the stream? The eagle soared under the invisible power of the wind. Could it be Bisbee was grounded by his shortsighted view of Charis? Perhaps the mystery of death was just as authentic as the realities of the visible world.

Lost in his thoughts, Bisbee stepped in a woodchuck hole and went tumbling down the hill. As he lay on his back in the soft alfalfa, he looked into the blue sky. Ignoring the fact that his ankle was beginning to swell, he began to softly weep. Surprised by the sudden release of buried emotions, hot tears ran down the sides of his face and filled his ears. He felt trapped between two worlds. If only he could talk to Avonlea. He envisioned her quietly listening to his dilemma. She always knew the words to say to make him feel better.

Living in the Land of Harness had become increasingly dangerous but at least it was familiar. His journey to this land called Charis was new territory for Bisbee. He was being forced to trust the Master on a deeper level. Change had always been difficult for Bisbee, and everything was changing so quickly it was making his head spin.

What or who would he find across the bridge? As he struggled to process this new information concerning death, his thoughts drifted and he lost all sense of time. The longer he laid in the clover field, the greater his doubts. Fear crept in, and with it, longings for home. Bisbee looked back up the hill.

Thinking back to the writings of Marnin, he realized life and death had been major themes. Is that what Marnin meant by death and life being in the same cup? Bisbee was tired and confused. Did the plague of the cave have something to do with a need to die? If he died, would he live again? He rolled it around in his mind until his brain hurt. The mental gymnastics exhausted him.

What if he decided to return to Harness? Would Marnin be disappointed? How would Avonlea respond if he returned home with no answers for their misery? He thought of his son and his passion for life. The same fire that burned in Avonlea burned in Stephen. When Stephen had asked to join his father on the journey to Charis, Avonlea was by his side, quietly nodding. Perhaps it would have been a good idea to include him. Stephen, for all his faults, was a man who knew how to take charge. Bisbee could use his help getting out of the clover.

Pain shot up Bisbee's leg causing him to grimace. As he lifted his head, he realized his ankle had swollen to twice its normal size. Anger surged through him as he dropped his head in the grass. Bisbee had always blamed others for his troubles, and in this case, a woodchuck was the culprit. Lifting his head, he looked toward Crossing Bridge.

"Great, I'll just limp into Charis. The Sojourner with a swollen ankle, the Pilgrim with the puffy foot."

He was about get up when he heard a voice behind him. But when he turned, Bisbee saw nothing but a distant cow pasture and a barbed wire fence separating him from it.

"I'm down here."

The voice was coming from somewhere in the clover field, but Bisbee saw nothing.

"Between the grass blades. You're thinking too big."

With his fingers, Bisbee separated the clover and there he stood, all four inches of him from tip to tail.

"You're a field mouse!"

Horatio C. Goldspinner

"Excellent observation, you are to be commended for your keen eye and intellectual capacity."

Bisbee did not know if he had been complimented or insulted. There was nothing in the expression of the mouse or vocal inflection to give him a hint as to the intention of his remark. After a short lick of his paws, the mouse continued.

"You appear as though you are in a pickle. Can I help you get up?"

"Sure, why not. This should be interesting."

"I've changed my mind. You are not to be commended for any degree of intelligence, my good man. Do you really think I could assist you in the least, seeing as I am a mouse and you are a massive human being?"

After a moment of silence, the lips of the mouse began to tense. Hitting the ground on all fours the little rodent began pounding his fists into the grass. Bisbee feared rabies.

Suddenly the mouse rolled over on his back convulsing with hysterical fits of laughter. Bisbee could only shake his head, and in spite of himself, he smiled.

Having recovered himself, the mouse stood back up and exchanged a more formal greeting with Bisbee.

"A pleasure to meet you. My name is Horatio C. Goldspinner, and you are in my field. Well, not that it's my field I suppose, I mean, well... on to the topic at hand, your clumsy descent down Ascending Hill. Quite the display of awkwardness, Bisbee."

Having never carried on a conversation with a field mouse and surprised that the rodent knew his name, all Bisbee could do was stare back at him. Horatio C. Goldspinner was an ordinary looking field mouse, except for the fact that he sported a red plaid blazer, which was nicely set off by a black silk bowtie. A pair of wire-framed glasses perched on the end of his nose, and a small but noticeable wart graced the left side of his face. Bisbee could not help noticing that half of Horatio's tail was missing.

"Cat got your tongue?" asked the field mouse.

Looking nervously left, and then right, Horatio continued.

"Oh! I do need to quit using that expression," the mouse exclaimed as he looked over his shoulder.

"The question you should be asking yourself at this moment in time, is not 'why did I step into the woodchuck hole,' but 'why am I walking down a hill when the name of the hill is Ascending?'"

Bisbee had overlooked the obvious conundrum, while focusing on his own internal struggle. Before meeting Horatio, this thought had not occurred to the Traveler. Why had he not questioned Marnin concerning the hill's name? He had been so focused on his inward pain that he had missed the first clue of Charis. Determined to pay more attention to details, Bisbee turned back toward Horatio.

"Alright, I give up," Bisbee said flatly. "Why am I descending down a hill called Ascending?"

Horatio straightened his bowtie.

"Not so fast. Marnin didn't send me to regurgitate predigested information into your mouth and down your gullet."

Bisbee was impressed.

"Wow, for a field mouse you have quite the vocabulary."

"Thank you but I shall not allow a well-deserved compliment to divert the attention off of the posed inquiry. I am patiently waiting for a well thought-out response to my original question, if you please."

Bisbee sat back and studied the little mouse. This must be his guide. He had expected someone bigger; someone human. What was the Master trying to teach him in this moment? Why send a field mouse?

"So you are my guide to Charis?"

"No, I am not your escort. However, my patience is wearing thin. I have an entire field to tend to, and I shall not be kept from it."

Horatio C. Goldspinner folded his arms, began tapping his foot, and stared intently into Bisbee's eyes. Feeling pressured, the Traveler began to ponder the riddle.

"Well, Mister Goldspinner, let's see, if the hill is named Ascending, and I am descending, then I am somehow in opposition to the hill."

Pleased with his answer, Bisbee smiled.

"Really? That's the best you've got? Try again," Horatio said.

Racking his brain, Bisbee felt a humiliation that one can only feel while standing in front of a mouse without an answer to a simple question.

"I should be walking back up the hill?

"No!"

"I should walk backward up the hill?"

"I can see this is going to be a long day. I'm not sure where you came from Bisbee, but it is obvious to me there was not a lot of free thinking going on there."

Bisbee thought back to Harness. The mouse was right. Thinking had always landed him in hot water with the Elders. They had preferred that he keep quiet and be submissive. Taking one more run at it, the Traveler hesitantly leaned forward.

"The way up is down?"

"Bingo! Rummy! Cash your chips in! Start the fireworks display! You've won the grand prize!"

The mouse was about to break into song when Bisbee interrupted him.

"But what does it mean?"

"It means my friend, the way into Charis is a descent, yet at the very moment you are moving downward, you are really moving upward. The way up is down because you are the strongest when you are the weakest, and you can only see when you realize that you are blind. You must carry nothing with you into Charis: no pride, no previous positions of honor, and no preconceived notions of life. You have much to learn, and Marnin only writes on a blank chalkboard."

Horatio C. Goldspinner's elegant speech had found its mark. Bisbee exhaled. Unaware that he still carried all those things, Bisbee wondered why it took a mouse in a field to bring it all to light.

"As for your fall into a woodchuck hole? It allowed you to meet me. Marnin orchestrated it to put you flat on your back, willing to listen to a creature you would not have given the time of day. Think of it, you might have crushed me under foot if not for your misstep and subsequent swollen ankle."

Bisbee realized how much he had to learn or unlearn. Rather than growing in confidence, the closer he got to Charis, the more deflated he became.

"Bisbee, you have been brought to Charis by a series of unfortunate events and experiences you would have never chosen for yourself. Marnin didn't cause these events, but he used them nonetheless. Even your swollen ankle will play a part in your journey."

As he turned to leave, Horatio C. Goldspinner looked back at Bisbee.

"You have a long way to go before you begin to understand what Marnin told you at the top of the hill. You will certainly face death in the land, but don't imagine in that moment you will understand what it means."

Bisbee was more confused than ever. Would he lose his personality, his unique sense of who he was, and how he related to other people? Was a robotic existence the Master's goal? Was it a mystical experience that would have little impact on his practical life? Horatio saw the gears turning in Bisbee's head and decided to shut them down.

"If you attempt to process the ramifications of death, with your rational mind, you will find yourself traveling down a dead end street. Take one step at a time, Bisbee. The way up is down."

Bisbee called after him.

"What happened to your tail?"

"Bitten off by a black snake. He desired more, but I was quicker. Be careful my friend."

"Black snakes aren't on my list of things that terrify me."

"Maybe you ought to put them on your list. Oh, by the way, say hello to my cousin." Before Bisbee could ask, Horatio C. Goldspinner disappeared into the clover.

Bisbee struggled to his feet and turned to face the valley. The fog had begun to lift, and the land before him came into full view. A herd of cows walked with him down the grassy road toward the bridge. Relaxed and chewing their cud, Bisbee wished he could be as calm as the gentle bovine.

Bisbee wondered where Horatio C. Goldspinner had gone. Buried in the grass, he could easily be crushed by any one of these careless cows. Bisbee chuckled: imagine being worried about the wellbeing of a field mouse.

Bisbee's swollen ankle looked up at him. It felt good not to be angry at the woodchuck anymore. He was somehow thankful for his fall.

No one purposely steps off a cliff. Our instinct to survive prevents us from leaping head first onto jagged rocks, inflicting pain with the possibility of fatality. We may speak glibly of death until we experience a brush with it. Feeling the cold fingers of death close by, we become aware of how much we desperately want to live. A man may not give consideration to his diet until his doctor tells him that what he is eating will soon kill him. Fruits and vegetables quickly become his daily delight.

In the physical realm, survival instinct is normal, but carried over into the Christian experience, it becomes a hindrance to growth. Self-preservation is not our friend: in the spiritual realm, death precedes life.

When Jesus speaks of discipleship, He bids us to individually take up our cross.[1] This type of discipleship calls, not for the fulfillment of our life, but for the end of it. The cross is ultimately an instrument of death, not suffering.

An old abandoned well was hidden next to the porch of my childhood home in Upstate New York. I would often push the top stone away and peer down into the wet, dark hole. The jagged rocks lining its walls were foreboding, and yet something beckoned me to enter and explore. I would imagine what it would be like to fall into its bottomless pit. Speed increasing with every passing moment, darkness enshrouding me, the smell of damp limestone piercing my nostrils, all added to the thrill of the imagined fall. Perhaps a sense of hopelessness would grip me as the seemingly never-ending journey continued into the blackness of despair.

Alas, I never worked up the nerve to anchor a rope and repel into the darkness. The uncertainty of what was in the well kept me at a distance. The thrill of the unknown was excitement enough.

When I first became a Christian, I immersed myself in the Bible. I carefully read the statements of Jesus concerning the cost of following Him. Even though I was clueless about its actual meaning, I was ready to lose my life and take up my cross. No sacrifice was too great in those early days of my pilgrimage. If taking up the cross involved the end of my life, well, so be it.

As is the case with new believers, my passion to obey my Lord outran my ability to understand what carrying my cross was really all about. Whatever Jesus meant when He said, "Take up your cross and follow me," fell on ears that were too young in the faith to comprehend.

Thus began my journey in the wilderness. By following the teachings of men, I bypassed the way of the cross. Working hard to perfect every phase of the Christian life, I labored to the point of exhaustion to prove my worth to Christ. Every Thursday night my attendance was counted at visitation. Diligent to follow the Lord with my best efforts, I left no stone unturned except the One that mattered.

Looking back, I took the easier path of embracing Christian disciplines as a means of growth. It just made more sense to my reasoning mind. The cross was replaced by the softer approach of developing good spiritual habits.

I do not regret those years; I now see them as a necessary step in my spiritual growth. It was a time of "wilderness wandering" and God used it to create in me a hunger for the Promised Land. Manna filled my belly but left me hungering for more. The promise of milk and honey gnawed at me. I needed something to stick to my bones.

For years, I simply treaded water to keep my head above the surface, always searching but never finding victory over sin. Every new approach to discipleship left me empty and disillusioned. I knew there must be more. I was convinced I was missing something; yet, I continued on, oblivious to all the warning signs. There were occasional blessings in the wilderness of human effort but no steady growth or victory.

One of the last results any patient wants to get from their doctor is that there is a blockage of blood flow. Whether the issue is cardiovascular, neurological, or something less dramatic, we want unrestricted circulation. Even a hand that has fallen asleep brings about concern. We adjust our bodies so that warm blood flows back into the paralyzed limb. As our hand comes "back to life," we breathe a sigh of relief. Blockages can sometimes be easily repaired. They can also be life threatening.

On our spiritual journey, growth is predicated on the flow of truth into our souls. The characteristics of a healthy spiritual life are revealed when we are ever learning and ever growing. When we neatly categorize new truth into the concrete mold labeled "suspicious," we can become stagnant in our growth. Because we have an established "grid" of spiritual interpretation, we can sometimes reject truth that could set us free. We should be careful to examine what is being "set" before us as truth. The refusal to be open to learning something new is evidence of a spiritual blockage.

Blockages can go on for years, undetected. Obstructions result in a crippling paralysis of the heart. The calcium deposits of dusty religious practice can build up until, one day, the "big one" hits. The "sin attack" can be as tragic as a colossal moral collapse (such as adultery) or as simple as becoming numb to the Lord.

The Israelites in the Old Testament lived in bondage for four hundred years. God, in His perfect timing, through His servant Moses, led them out of Egypt toward the Promise Land of Canaan. The future appeared bright as they approached the land flowing with milk and honey. Spies were sent in to bring back a report of all they saw. For forty days they searched out the land. When the spies returned, they brought a giant cluster of grapes that took two men to carry. In giving their report, they all agreed that the land did indeed flow with milk and honey.

Then everything went wrong. The giants in the land dominated the thinking of ten out of the twelve spies.[2] The people of Israel were warned not to enter. The ten spies claimed that the walled cities were an insurmountable barrier to victory. Saying that they felt like "tiny grasshoppers" before the inhabitants of the land, they sent fear into the hearts of their brethren. What had appeared as a bright future for the descendants of Abraham became, in their eyes, a suicide mission. Their entire focus was taken off of Jehovah and placed on themselves. Their perspective was no longer the greatness of God, who could surely give them the land; the attention was now shifted to the power of the enemy. Instead of trusting in an all-powerful God, they became cowards before finite men.

Where did they go wrong? Where was the fork in the road, causing the Israelites to end up back in the wilderness for forty years? We are quick to blame the ten spies, but perhaps the point of deviation occurred earlier.

God had commanded Moses to send in spies in order to search out the land. That is all He told him to do, nothing more. No further instructions were given; just go look. Apparently that was not enough for Moses. After receiving this clear and simple command, he went to work creating a rubric for the spies to follow.[3] It was Moses who led them down the wrong path.

The twelve spies were given a checklist of questions concerning the land and its inhabitants. Were the people of Canaan strong or weak? How many were there? Was it a good land? Were the cities walled or without fortifications? Was the land rich or poor? How was the timber supply? Six questions in all were to be answered by the spies. It was a devilish census, taken for the purpose of human assessment. Human reasoning had entered the equation of conquest, and the slope became very slippery. When God makes a promise, it is not time to calculate.

Numbers are of great significance in the Bible. It is interesting that the number six is the number for mankind, and seven is the number for divine perfection. Moses desired answers to six questions instead of believing the promise of God. The Land of Canaan was theirs for the taking. God had promised that the land flowed with milk and honey.[4] Instead of believing and marching forward, they calculated and stopped dead in their tracks. The rubric of human reasoning ruined them.

The spies were sent into the Promise Land from the wilderness of *Paran*.[5] The root word for *Paran* in the Hebrew language is to embellish or boast. It means to add something to the message. The spies were not to assess the possibility of conquest; they were supposed to bring back a report of what they saw. In light of the promises of God, Moses should have boldly led the people into their inheritance, but instead he did what religious folk have done since the beginning of time. He decided to help God by using his reasoning mind.

To my fellow pastors, have you ever felt the need to give the church a plan, a rubric? It may sound trite or overworked to tell a congregation to just "wait on the Lord," but that is what the Scripture tells us to do. For years, I labored under the assumption that the work of building His church was on my shoulders. The greatest gift a spiritual leader can give a group of believers is to point to the Savior and then stay out of the way.

The message of the cross is clear: life is only found in death. The message of grace becomes muddy when we add the checklist of human effort. Human reasoning is our greatest enemy as we approach an understanding of grace. It is what we "know" that creates the blockages that become lethal. The heart slows its beat and the brain hemorrhages. What we need is by-pass surgery. All our rationale must be by-passed.

The chalkboards of our minds can become so filled with the methods of men that there is no room left for the truth that truly liberates. The way up is down, and it is only when we confess our blindness that we begin to see the truth.

By taking up our cross, we are saying "goodbye" to a life lived by our own meager power and ability. Grace is a rejection of the calculating mind of man. It is a declaration of our complete dependence on Christ, leaving us with no credit for battles won. We do not "do" anything; He has already won the victory! In Romans 3:27, Paul asked, "Where is boasting?" The Apostle then answers with quiet resolution, "It is excluded."

The choice is simple. Remain in a law-based form of man-made religion, touting human effort as the basis of growth or enter a life lived purely by the grace of God. Either stay in the wilderness of attempting to "live for Jesus" or enter the land of milk and honey, which is, "His life in you." A refusal to cross over is really a denial of the full inheritance that He died to give you.

The choice is yours; continue to live on dry crackers or begin to enjoy a sweeter fare. The old wood-plank bridge awaits those who are tired and hungry. In the land of grace, milk and honey are in full supply.

CHAPTER 4

CROSSING BRIDGE

As Bisbee approached the creek, he saw the old wooden plank bridge stretching its span. The melodic song of the stream, flowing over the rocks, comforted him. A large weeping willow stood majestically beside the bridge, shading it from the morning sun. Its low hanging branches gently kissed the waters as they swayed in the breeze. Suddenly, an old crow screamed from its branches, with warning cries that sounded almost human.

"Go back, go back!"

Bisbee smiled. He had come too far to turn back now.

The Traveler sat down in the shade of the willow and placed his swollen ankle in the cool water. He thought about the field mouse and his fall in the woodchuck hole. He knew Horatio Goldspinner was right. If he continued to dwell on his own personal struggles, he would miss Charis. Choosing to put aside his internal strife, he began to reflect on the events Marnin had used to lead him to this bridge.

As he stared into the stream, a painful memory clawed its way to the surface of Bisbee's mind. Unable to send the unwelcomed intruder back into the recesses of his mind, it crawled out and sat down next to him by the creek. The Traveler shuttered as he recalled the night Stephen was brought home: bloody and at death's door. While walking down a country road, late one night, Stephen had been gored by one of the Beasts and left for dead in a ditch outside of town.

Seeing his son lying unconscious on the kitchen table in a puddle of blood was the most terrifying moment of Bisbee's life. Slipping in and out of consciousness, Stephen asked the same question over and over.

"Why?"

The question haunted Bisbee. Why could the Beasts not be conquered?

In his son's eyes, Bisbee had seen anguish and fear. The pain the Beasts had inflicted on Stephen went far beyond the physical realm. It wounded his mind and soul. After his brush with death, Stephen found it difficult to go out at night. Still able to function during the day, Stephen struggled to sleep each night. Occasionally waking in a cold sweat, he relived the painful thrust of the Beast's sharp tusk into his flesh. Neither Bisbee nor his son would ever be the same.

Holding Stephen in his arms, he had experienced a level of hatred for the Beasts he had never known before. The night came and went, but Bisbee never forgot the pain Stephen had endured. He placed a portion of the blame on himself. Bisbee could not change a decision made long ago, but why did he feel powerless to move in a different direction? If only he had not brought his family to Harness, then none of this would have happened.

Driven to obsession, he began sharing his concerns with Marnin. The Master was strangely quiet about Bisbee's anger and confusion. No matter how many times he brought it up, Marnin would just patiently listen. Could it be there was a greater purpose in what had happened that night? Had his son's brush with death been a calling of sorts, an awakening? Perhaps the unwelcomed stranger, sitting next Bisbee under the willow, was a necessary evil.

Horatio C. Goldspinner was right. Marnin had used a moment of horror in Bisbee's life; a memory that was so awful he longed to bury it in the deepest ocean. Bisbee's journey to Charis had really begun on the night Stephen almost died.

Bisbee was surprised by an emotion that had attached itself to the memory of that night. Gratitude, like a tugboat, was mooring up against the wreckage and was slowly pulling it safely into harbor. Tied securely to the Dock of Purpose, the Damaged Vessel would never be repaired, but at least Bisbee had begun to understand its place in the grand scheme of life. He realized Marnin had nothing to do with his son's brush with death, but in some mysterious way, he had been able to use the experience to open Bisbee's eyes.

There were other less dramatic moments, Bisbee recalled as he sat by the creek, but none so life altering as the night he almost lost his son. No wonder Stephen had wanted to join him in this journey to Charis.

As the waters passed over his feet, he thought about his family back home. Once the Elders had discovered he was missing, an official inquiry would have taken place. Had Bisbee placed his loved ones in danger? How did Stephen respond to the Elders when they came to their home? Bisbee was afraid for his family.

In the midst of his doubts, a dragonfly flew past and landed on a small branch, just above his head. As he looked up at the tiny creature, Bisbee wished he could grab its wings and fly back home. The water-dipper danced from branch to branch and then suddenly turned and winked at Bisbee. What kind of journey was this, where field mice speak and dragonflies wink?

Bisbee's trance under the willow was interrupted by a splashing sound behind him. He turned to see a strange sight: a muskrat, dripping wet from head to toe and sporting a sheepish grin. Looking Bisbee over, the muskrat made no effort to conceal his excitement.

Charlie the muskrat

"So you are Bisbee. Marnin said you were coming."

Bisbee could only stare.

"Allow me to introduce myself. We haven't much time. Charlie is the name, and I am your personal guide."

Why was Bisbee surprised? Well, at least a muskrat was an upgrade from a field mouse, he thought. Even so, he had hoped for a more impressive guide. Not *that he had anything against muskrats. All he really knew about them was... well he didn't know anything about them.*

Bisbee looked Charlie over, inspecting him as if he were a new calf. From his round, chubby shape, he concluded that Charlie had not missed too many meals. The creek was obviously filled with unsuspecting game, which the muskrat feasted on at will. Covered with brown fur, his two protruding front teeth reminded Bisbee of an old cartoon character. He decided not to mention the noticeable wound on the muskrat's left leg. After all, Bisbee was sporting quite a wound himself.

"I knew it... disappointed." Charlie remarked. The perceptive creature had read Bisbee's face.

"No, I mean not really. I am a little surprised that Marnin would choose a muskrat."

Bisbee struggled to talk his way out of this awkward moment. He was thankful to have a guide, even if it was another rodent. Bisbee was learning the Master was fond of using humble means to accomplish his plans.

"Disappointed or not, I'm your muskrat. If you have a complaint, I suggest you take it up with the powers that be; but for now, let's get going. You've got a lot to unlearn."

Where had he heard that before? As Charlie turned toward the bridge, Bisbee hesitated. This was the moment he had been warned about in Harness. The old, wooden plank bridge that crossed over into Charis had been portrayed as weak and unreliable. Bisbee studied the wooden planks. Strangely the bridge looked sturdy. How many lies had he been told by the Elders? Had it been intentional or did they know what they were doing?

Bisbee looked across the stream into the Land of Charis. Lush, green grass grew in the fields, and trees budded with fresh leaves. Charis was more beautiful than he had imagined. Why did the Elders discredit this amazing place? The Leaders of Harness actually taught that Charis was the breeding ground of the Beasts. No proof of this assertion was ever offered, and no challenge was ever made to the claim.

Charlie walked a few more steps before he realized that Bisbee was not following. The muskrat stopped and turned around.

"I know what they told you. It's not true, you know." Charlie had read the moment perfectly.

"Great, the muskrat can read my thoughts," Bisbee muttered to himself. "This should make for an interesting partnership."

Bisbee stared into the ground.

"No, it's not that."

"Well, what is it?" asked Charlie. The muskrat looked into Bisbee's eyes with intensity.

"Has the Master led you to this bridge?" Charlie inquired.

"Yes." Bisbee replied confidently.

"Do I see a map and are those writings I see in your hand?"

"Yes, they are."

Bisbee began to see his point.

"Then why aren't you following me across the bridge? Are you going to listen to Marnin and follow the map and the writings, or are you going to follow the voices of men, filling your head with teachings that keep you in bondage and fear?"

Bisbee had underestimated his guide. Underneath all that matted brown fur and behind those bucked teeth was a creature that trusted Marnin completely. It was humbling to be reproached by a muskrat.

"Are you coming? Marnin has no pleasure in those who turn back after seeing Crossing Bridge."

Bisbee took one more look up the hill. As he turned back toward the muskrat, a smile crept across his face.

"Let's go!"

With his first step toward the bridge, Bisbee discovered a confidence and assurance he had never known before. Faith had replaced doubt, and he knew before he ever stepped onto the first plank that he was heading in the right direction. Gone were the voices of his past. Armed with the map and the writings, led by a muskrat, Bisbee stepped onto the first wooden plank.

The crossing had begun.

As his right foot pressed into the first wooden plank, he anticipated weakness, but he found it to be quite strong. The old timbers were as solid as a rock. In a matter of moments, he was on the other side. Bisbee hardly recalled his footsteps as the planks rattled firmly under his feet. It reminded him of the moment he had decided to follow Marnin. How quickly it all took place. How powerful a moment can be, he thought?

With the sound of the stream behind him, he looked down at the ground beneath him. Bisbee was instantly overwhelmed by new discoveries. The first thing he noticed was how solid the ground felt. Setting the map and the writings down, Bisbee leapt into the air. Amazed at the firmness of his landing, he jumped until he was exhausted. The ground in Harness had been soft and uneven. It was no wonder his footing was always giving him trouble. He understood now why his legs ached at the end of each day. It had been exhausting to walk in the tiresome landscape of Harness. The stable footing in this new land astounded him.

The air was lighter in Charis, easier to breathe, and carried with it a sweet aroma. Bisbee closed his mouth and let the air fill his nostrils. The Beasts had so polluted the atmosphere in Harness that breathing had become difficult. It felt good to fill his lungs with air that did not choke him. He looked back up Ascending Hill and at the top of it sat Marnin, smiling. Bisbee looked around for Charlie.

"I'm right here."

He looked down to see his new friend, dripping wet and holding a crawfish in his mouth.

"I thought we were crossing the bridge together," Bisbee protested.

"I'm your guide, not your partner. Crossing over is something you had to do alone and besides I was hungry."

"So let me get this straight, your stomach comes before my safety?" Bisbee quipped.

Charlie just smiled and tossed a claw into the bushes. Bisbee returned his smile and continued.

"I wish my family was here to celebrate the moment."

"It's a very personal thing, Bisbee. Crossing over into this land is such a special moment, Marnin has chosen it to be a private occasion. They will know soon enough."

Charlie offered Bisbee the remains of the crawfish. Trying not to look disgusted, Bisbee declined.

His mind wandered back to the Elders.

"Lies, Charlie, they were all lies. This land isn't a breeding ground for the Beasts. Why did they tell us that? Why haven't more crossed over? Their lies have kept more from crossing over."

"The Elders fear this land, Bisbee. They have no control over the lives of others in this place. Here, Marnin is supreme, and shares his place of honor with

no one. It's easier to create lies born out of willful ignorance, than to point others to this land of freedom. The Elders of Harness secretly love their place of honor. Unwilling to relinquish control over the lives of those who live in Harness, they slander Charis. Besides, you have to be ready to walk away from it all, my friend. Most simply turn around, and go back to Harness."

Bisbee looked confused.

"You mean others have come to this bridge and turned back?"

"More than I can count." Charlie's eyes wandered back up the hill as a sadness swept over his face.

"I had doubts about you, but alas, it is done and you have chosen well, my new friend. You have rejected the shallow voices of men in favor of the solid words of Marnin. You have entered the Land of Charis, and your adventure is before you."

Bisbee felt as light as a feather; excitement surged through him like soft lightning. He thought of his family back in Harness, and how exciting it would be to send them news of Charis. As Bisbee stood by the bridge, Charlie turned and began walking up the path.

"Aren't you forgetting something?" asked Charlie.

Bisbee looked back and saw the map and the writings lying on the ground next to the bridge. As he walked back to retrieve them, he noticed the herd of cows had gathered at the fence. The bovine stared at Bisbee with accusatory eyes. As he gathered the parchments, a surprising sense of shame entered the Traveler. Why had he left the writings behind?

Crossing over into a life lived by the grace of God is a huge event. It resembles light breaking in on the soul. The moment of discovery usually occurs in a time of quiet desperation, and even though our heart celebrates wildly, the fanfare and applause of others is rare. Tired and bone weary from the pressure of religion, we collapse into the arms of Jesus. Out of breath and unwilling to try anymore to please God, we finally reach an end of our efforts to win His approval. It is a moment we share alone with our Heavenly Father, safe within His embrace. Resting in His grace alone, we are finally free.

But free from what? It's an important question, but before we answer it, let's look at the internal struggle involved in bringing us to the place where we cross over into grace.

From our earliest memories, we were taught to be independent. We were strongly encouraged to tie our own shoes, comb our own hair, and to make our own way in this world. As childhood gave way to adolescence, we looked forward to being on our own. It was exciting to think about making our own decisions and choosing our own path. We made mistakes, but along the way we learned from them. In the process of growing to maturity, we established our independence.

In our present world, all this is considered good and normal.

However, in the spiritual life, we have entered a realm where human effort and intellectual maneuvering become hindrances to grace. Even more than hindrances, they become the very fountain of failure. Evan H. Hopkins writes concerning the believers' attempts to live the Christian life according to effort. "Many have a true aim, seeking to glorify Christ and to be made like Him-they have sincere and earnest desires, and they are making constant and vigorous efforts after holiness-and yet they are continually being disappointed. Failure and defeat meet them at every turn. Not because they do not try, not because they do not struggle-they do all this-but because the life they are living is essentially the *self-life* and not the *Christ-life*."[1]

As a small boy, growing up in the country, I once passed by a dead cow lying in a pasture. She had been deceased for some time and was bloated. As I stood at the fence admiring the ever- expanding girth of the cow, now twice its normal size, an old farmer passed by and gave me a warning.

"Look all you want, boy, just don't stick a pitchfork in her." I took his advice and walked away. The thought of the sickening odor that would fill the air once she was punctured was enough to send me down the road.

Paul addresses three types of pride in the early chapters of Romans. First, he writes concerning self-loathing pride, which causes a man to never see himself worthy of the grace of God.[2] Next he targets intellectual pride, which demands a full understanding of a truth before it can be embraced.[3] Finally, as if speaking of his own past experience,

Paul exposes religious pride.[4] This type of pride always establishes a system of works in order to please God. All three types are equally and deservedly under the crown of grace. God's grace, hurdles our minds, pushes past our unworthiness, and trumps our efforts, but He never forces grace on us. It is still our choice to come out from behind these weak and fractured facades. To cling to any of these three prideful barriers, is to refuse God's grace and remain barricaded in pride's putrefying fortification.

Listen carefully to these statements:

"He died for me, so I could live for Him."

"When our praises go up, His blessings come down."

"The reason you aren't being blessed is you have sin in your life."

Do you see the common root of these pulpit imperatives? Spoken from well-respected platforms or around water coolers at work, these statements first appear as powerful motivational mantras. Dig a little deeper into their source, and you will find yourself drowning in the rotten cesspool of man's pride. Like the bloating cow, human effort looks impressive, but plunge a pitchfork into its carcass, and you will vomit from the stench.

According to Ephesians 2:13, we are made close (nigh) by the blood of Christ. The Scripture does not say that we have been brought close by our efforts. Neither does it state that we have to maintain this amazing closeness by our devotions. Furthermore, we are not waiting to get to heaven before we enjoy this intimacy. We have been made nigh, once and for all time, by the blood of Christ. The Greek word for "nigh" in this verse is *"eggus"*, and it means to squeeze. If God squeezes me, man or ministry cannot bring me any closer.

Look honestly at the clear statements of the Bible. According to Ephesians 1:3, we have been blessed with *all* spiritual blessings in Christ. How can my faithfulness or devotion bring blessings if I already possess them by virtue of my settled position in Christ? Therefore, the idea that I can now live for Christ by his aid and or help is pleasing to the ears but actually imprisons the soul. We are held captive in this legalistic approach by our pride.

The walk down the hill toward a life of grace can take a long time. The debate raging within can last for weeks, months, even years.

Pride is a deceitful taskmaster. It is possible to lay in the soft alfalfa for a long time, chewing over in our minds the implication of abandoning ourselves to grace. Something within us wants to play a part in the process of our sanctification. We want to fulfill our responsibility to the Lord; it just makes sense. The end of our efforts and struggle violates all human reasoning.

In almost all of Paul's epistles, he first establishes the believers' position in Christ. In Ephesians, he pulls back the curtain in heaven and reveals the sitting position of the Christian.[5] Being seated is a posture of rest, from which we are to remain. Paul then tells the believer to "walk."[6] How am I to walk if I am sitting? We are to walk from a sitting position. Finally, Paul tells the soldier of Christ to "stand" against the enemy.[7] As we are seated in Christ, we walk according to His power, and as a result, the devil attacks. Our response is to stand against him, being clothed with the armor of God. Notice, it is not armor *from* God but the armor *of* God Himself.

The bridge we must pass over into God's abundant life leaves behind all effort on our part and urges us to simply rest in Christ. It dramatically shifts our paradigm of thinking about the Christian life. Instead of what we must do to be close to God, the approach of grace tells us we are already close to Him by what He has done for us in Christ. Instead of pulling the strings of heaven by an effective prayer life, we see ourselves seated in the heavenly places in Christ. Rather than seeing our lives as fulfilled by Jesus, we view ourselves crucified, buried, and then raised from the dead. Paul tells us in Colossians 3:3 that we are dead and our life has been hidden with Christ in God.

There is no greater deathblow to pride than crossing over into a walk of full reliance on His mercy and grace.

The children of Israel spent forty years in the desert learning one central truth; by our strength we cannot enter the Promise Land. An entire generation had to die before they were ready to enter. Only Joshua and Caleb trusted the Lord. This pair of warriors rejected human reasoning and their own strength for God's full provision. The rest of the nation of Israel had to learn through the bitterness of death to fully trust in the Lord to fight their battles.

Every ounce of human reasoning and self-effort must die. If it takes forty years in a desert, then so be it. The Lord is in no hurry. He will not take any part of you into this land of grace. Paul told the Galatians that if they succumbed to circumcision, they were obligated to do the whole law, and as a result, Christ would profit them nothing.[8]

When Paul reached the end of chapter seven, in the Book of Romans, he came to a life-altering conclusion.[9] In his efforts to keep the law, he discovered to his amazement, an utter inability to produce obedience. He concluded that he was dead to the law that he might live unto God. There is no part of weakness left in a dead man. Death is the extremity of weakness. A weak man may still try, but a dead man puts forth no effort.

All hope that you can please God must be abandoned. He awaits your end before beginning His work. Watchmen Nee wrote this, "Being fully persuaded that we cannot do it, we cease trying to please God from the ground of the old man. Having at last reached the point of utter despair in ourselves so that we cease even to try, we put our trust in the Lord to manifest His resurrected life in us."[10]

Jesus asked a very simple question to the worshippers of his day in the seventh chapter of the Gospel of John.[11] He stood and cried out, "Are you thirsty?" He still asks the same question today.

CHAPTER 5

BACK HOME

The long, anticipated knock on the front door brought a sense of relief to Avonlea. Before she ever turned its rusty knob, she knew who would be standing on the other side. Avonlea calmly opened the door. Three Elders stood on her narrow front porch with expressionless faces. Dripping wet from an unexpected summer storm, they appeared to have had a bit of their dignity washed away by the thick and steady raindrops. Avonlea fought back a smile.

From the corner of her eye, she spotted Stephen standing in the side yard. Holding a pitchfork that was pointed skyward, her son was glaring at the men. She quickly ushered them inside.

It was an unusual sight indeed to have such men visit a humble dwelling like theirs; yet these were unusual times. Bisbee's departure had caused quite a stir in their small community. His journey to Charis had fanned the flames of rebellion throughout Harness. What had smoldered in the hearts of his countrymen had caught fire. The inhabitants of Harness were no longer content to live in the shadow of the Beasts. The people of Harness wanted more, and unbeknownst to Bisbee, he was slowly becoming their hero.

As the three men stood stoically in her front living room, Avonlea restrained the anger she knew would ruin the chances of a satisfying encounter. She could not remember a single visit the Elders had ever made to their home in all the years they had lived in Harness. One of the Beasts had almost killed Stephen earlier that year, and yet none of the leaders of Harness had cared enough to come and check on him. The thought agitated Avonlea.

"I think you know why we are here."

"Why don't you enlighten me," snarled Avonlea.

Through the pain of past experiences with Bisbee's wife, the Elders knew they were walking into a bobcat's den but their need of information was greater than their fear of being clawed to death.

"Is he here?"

"Who? Stephen? You didn't see him in the yard, pitchfork in hand?"

The Elders glanced nervously at one another. Macafee, the Chief Elder, tensed his lips and locked his eyes on Avonlea.

"Bisbee? Is he here?"

"You wouldn't be here if he was." Avonlea responded without turning her eyes away from Macafee.

Suddenly, a loud clap of thunder rocked the house, causing the Elders to brace themselves. Avonlea continued to stare at Macafee, unaffected by the loud blast.

Hearing the commotion, Lorelai appeared from her bedroom. Standing timidly in the doorway, fear spread like wild fire across her young face. Avonlea, noticing her presence, motioned for her to return to her room. Though normally compliant, Lorelai remained in the doorway, refusing to obey. Bisbee's bride turned back toward Macafee.

"You know he's not here. All of you should have seen this coming. How long did you think we could go on living this charade? The terror of the Beasts is growing, and you seem unable or unwilling to stop them. I would have thought that you would have led the expedition to defeat them: yet here you are, questioning me."

Avonlea waited for her last statement to take hold, but Macafee's face refused to yield.

"Bisbee will find the answers we seek and when he returns, your control over Harness will be broken. He has gone to Charis... but you already knew that, didn't you?"

Macafee looked away.

"Why do you cringe when I say Charis? What is it about that land that terrifies you? Whatever it is, we refuse to live any longer in fear. We reject your authority in our lives. When Bisbee returns, and he will, we will follow him to Charis. This house will be as vacant as your empty heart."

Avonlea had never been short on words. She had always known how to get to the heart of a matter and once there, had no hesitation performing the surgery she felt necessary, without the use of anesthesia. The marks of the bobcat were evident on Macafee's face.

"I had hoped to come and reason with you, Avonlea."

"You may call me Mrs. Saxton."

"Mrs. Saxton it is. Reports have come to us that your husband is close to the land called ... that land. We have sent a man to bring him home."

"You don't know Bisbee, do you? He won't listen to him."

Avonlea stepped forward.

"The fire that burns in his heart, burns in ours. It is the desire to be free."

"You are all making a terrible mistake, Mrs. Saxton."

"The only mistake would be to continue to live in fear when we know something better is awaiting us in Charis."

"Think about what you are sacrificing. Harness is all that your children have ever known. Is uprooting them worth it to you? This is where your friends live. Who do you know in that land?"

Emboldened by a sudden flash of anger, Avonlea gripped the chair in front of her.

"The roots in Harness are shallow. They are constantly being trampled and torn by the Beasts that ruin any hope of real relationships. You speak of sacrifice as if it were something you actually know about. Our visit is over. You should go."

Feeling the abrasiveness of the brick wall he faced, Macafee turned to leave. Tourgen, one of the Elders, walked close to Avonlea and slipped a small piece of paper into her hand. As he leaned in even closer, he whispered in her ear.

"Give this to Stephen."

Squeezing the note tight in her hand, she watched the three men walk toward the front door. Once outside, Macafee turned back toward Avonlea.

"You'll regret this day."

"No, I think you will."

All Avonlea heard after that was the creaking of the wooden steps. The Elders walked past two large lilacs and down the trail, back toward the center of town.

Turning back into the house, Avonlea found Lorelai, sitting on her bed. She was staring into the floorboards.

"Why did he have to go, Mother? What is so bad about Harness? Father has ruined our lives."

Avonlea should have known this was coming. She had been so preoccupied with the pressure under which she was living since Bisbee left, that she had been caught off guard. She knew that Lorelai enjoyed deep friendships and as a result, was willfully blind to the danger of the Beasts. Harness was all that the young girl had ever known and change had always been a dreaded proposition for Lorelai. Placing her arm around her daughter, she spoke softly.

"I know this is hard. I know you don't like change. But…"

"But what? We pack up and leave? We move to a land we have never seen and live with strangers?"

"Lorelai, we can't go on living in Harness. Your brother almost died last spring. You watched him bleed on that kitchen table."

Avonlea pointed into the other room.

"But I have friends here."

Avonlea reached out to take Lorelai's hand, but the young girl turned away.

"It's the Miller boy, isn't it, the one with the beard?"

Lorelai rose and walked toward the window.

"Yes."

Avonlea placed her hand softly on Lorelai's shoulder.

"Honey, how do you know Merkel isn't ready to leave Harness?"

"I don't."

Silently staring into the distant cornfield, she seemed to Avonlea to be out of reach. Knowing that further discussion would only push her away, Avonlea left her to her thoughts. This was something Lorelai would have to figure out for herself. Avonlea knew it was more than just the Miller boy that was keeping her from Charis.

Sitting down at the kitchen table Avonlea unraveled the note Tourgen had placed in her hand. Her eyes widened, as she tightened her hand back around the small piece of paper and stared out the window. Stephen was walking toward the house. Speaking as if to herself, she barely muttered the words.

"And so it begins."

CHAPTER 6

HUGABONE

Charlie looked down and noticed Bisbee's swollen ankle had begun to turn blue.

"Your ankle needs attention. Let's walk back down to the stream. The cold water will reduce the swelling."

They turned and headed back down the trail toward the creek.

Bisbee was moved by Charlie's compassion. In the excitement of passing over the bridge, he had forgotten all about his injury. It seemed like moments ago he had been tumbling down Ascending Hill. Bisbee wanted to ask Charlie about his wounded leg but decided to wait.

Suddenly with great excitement, a sparrow flew past.

"Hugabone's coming, Hugabone's coming."

The frantic bird flew into the willow tree. Startled and confused, Bisbee looked down at Charlie.

A look of terror overtook the muskrat's face. Bisbee had already become accustomed to Charlie's happy, carefree spirit, and so it was difficult to see his little friend in such obvious distress. Without speaking a word, Charlie ran to the bridge and slid quietly under its thick wooden planks. Bisbee followed the muskrat to the edge of the bridge. Upstream, he could hear the sound of limbs being broken. As a figure approached, he wondered if it would be wise to join Charlie under the bridge.

Bisbee watched with great interest, as an old man climbed over a rusty barbed wire fence and rounded a bend. Too late to hide and too curious to run, Bisbee stood frozen on the bank. After a slight pause, the stranger fought through some mulberry bushes and appeared on the opposite side of the stream. Having *slid down the muddy bank, he stood directly under the willow and stared up at Bisbee. The sparrow flew down at the stranger, which caused him to stumble on the smooth rocks.*

"Get outta here you stupid bird."

After he had regained his composure, he renewed his look of interrogation.

"You lost?"

Bisbee was speechless. Did he look lost? He had not checked the map or the writings since entering Charis, but had he been in the land long enough to get lost?

Bisbee decided he would ignore the question, based solely on the old man's ridiculous appearance. Dressed in ragged army fatigues, that should have been discarded long ago, he seemed to be the type of man who had been discharged from the military against his will. His feet pointed outward, and he was slightly stooped over. He appeared intimidating and comical, all at the same time. His greying blonde hair poked wildly out from under an old army cap, and the bushy hair on the back of his neck had grown so thick that it could be seen from a distance. In his left hand was a trap, hanging from an old rusty chain, and over his right shoulder hung a leather sack, dripping wet. Bisbee thought he saw something move inside the bag.

"Well, boy, you gonna answer my question or just stand there with that stupid look on your face?"

The old man cocked his head sideways and waited for a response. Slowly chewing on a wad of tobacco, bulging from his left cheek, he spat into the water. Thick, brown juice ran down his chin and dripped onto his jacket. In his struggle to process the moment, Bisbee did not know whether to run or laugh. Finally, the Traveler stepped forward.

Hugabone

"No sir, I know exactly where I am."

Bisbee was surprised at his own boldness.

"Well, you look lost. Got a name?"

"Bisbee, the name's Bisbee."

"I heard you the first time. I may be old, but I ain't deaf. What are you doing in these parts?"

Bisbee had not expected to meet such a man in Charis. Of course, the old man was not exactly in Charis, but he was walking its border. He remembered Marnin's warning and decided to be coy. Walking out onto the bridge, Bisbee sat down on the dry planks. After pausing to stare into the stranger's eyes, he decided to engage the trapper.

"Just out for a walk. You know, pretty day and all."

The old trapper pulled a ragged photo from his shirt pocket. He studied it for a few moments and then lifted his eyes to look at Bisbee. After having released a long stream of brown tobacco juice into the water, he slid it back in his pocket.

"Out for a walk, huh?"

"That's right."

"Well, you ain't hiding a muskrat round here, are ya?"

"Muskrat? Looking for a muskrat?" Bisbee asked.

The trapper glanced at his traps and then turned back toward Bisbee.

"You a quick study, boy. Must of made it to the eighth grade."

Bisbee hated sarcasm. His father had always discouraged the practice. The Traveler frowned, stood up, and brushed off his pants.

"Well, sir, we are not going to have a productive conversation if you intend on insulting me."

The trapper snarled and spat again.

Bisbee knew Charlie was in danger, and the last thing he needed was to lose his guide, besides he was growing fond of the muskrat. What was a man like this doing stomping around Living Stream? Charis was turning out to be more wild and dangerous than he had anticipated. Attempting to divert the conversation, he asked the stranger his name.

"Hugabone. Hezzy Hugabone."

"Well, Mr. Hugabone, I wouldn't be caught dead with a muskrat. Slimy little rodents, if you ask me."

Bisbee was pleased with his quick response, but movement under the bridge quickened his heart rate.

"Well, the pelts of those slimy little rodents fetch a pretty penny at the market," Hugabone explained. "Besides, I kind of enjoy seeing 'em thrash about with their leg caught in my trap."

The old man's cracked lips formed a twisted smile. What teeth he had left were brown and rotten. Bisbee was sickened by the thought of Hugabone's pleasure in seeing an animal in torment. He understood why Charlie was hiding under the bridge.

The trapper was about to speak when Bisbee saw movement in the leather sack.

"So what's in the bag?"

Hugabone swung the sack around. "You ain't real smart, are ya?"

"Well, my guess would be a muskrat." Bisbee replied.

"Oh, a real col-lee-ga-ga-ite-ti."

"You mean collegiate man?"

"Whatever. Smart alec."

Bisbee smiled and pointed back to Hugabone's sack.

"Looks kind of small, though."

Hugabone appeared irritated. "Nothing's small about this one, she's a good four pounds."

"Looks more like a two pounder to me."

"Stupid city slicker."

Hugabone reached in the sack and pulled the muskrat out by its feet. Dazed and confused, the animal spun around in an attempt to get its bearings. Blood ran down it's leg, soaking its soft pelt.

"She's a beaut, ain't she?"

"I can't tell its weight when it's hanging upside down."

Hugabone spat into the water. Agitated by Bisbee's inquiries, the trapper slowly reached around the back of the muskrat. In the very moment that Hugabone grabbed the animal's neck, the muskrat came alive. Her eyes bulged as she let out a blood-curdling scream. With lightning speed, she sunk her sharp teeth into Hugabone's left arm. The trapper cried out in agony, as he dropped his catch into the fast flowing stream. As the muskrat swam to safety, Hugabone turned back toward Bisbee.

"Think you're smart, don't ya?"

Bisbee held back a smile. "Maybe a little smarter than you."

"Well, if you've got half a brain, you'll go back to Harness where you belong."

A look of confusion spread across Bisbee's face.

"You've heard of Harness? Who are you anyway?"

"That's not important, boy."

Hugabone pulled the picture out of his pocket and waved it in Bisbee's face. "Recognize him?"

Shocked, Bisbee took the photo from Hugabone.

"How did you get this?"

"The Elders gave it to me. How does it feel to be a wanted man?"

Hugabone paused long enough to enjoy Bisbee's reaction and then continued.

"If you stay in this land beyond the bridge, you will be lost to Harness forever. You will be seen as a traitor to your people. Bisbee, you're a fool if you don't return."

"You're lying old man! Show me proof."

Hugabone pulled a worn parchment from his back pocket and began to read.

"Anyone who enters Charis will be declared unclean and labeled as a traitor. Those who even speak of Charis will be branded a 'Tzaraath'."

"As we speak, Bisbee, a sign hangs outside the door of your house, 'The dwelling of a Tzaraath.' Your son is burning with fever and will soon die. No one has contact with your family. Because of your selfish journey to Charis, your loved ones have been cut off from the Meeting Place."

Bisbee fell to one knee, his head spinning. He couldn't believe what he had heard. He knew that there would be trouble when he left, but he never imagined it would go this far. Bisbee thought of Avonlea, and the pain that she must be enduring. He had left her alone and unprotected. Hugabone took his silence as an invitation to continue.

"Your leaving has caused the people of Harness to question the wisdom of the Elders. If you don't return soon, an uprising will occur, destroying your family and all of Harness."

Hugabone looked into the eyes of Bisbee and saw a man that was bending to his point of view. Hugabone's ability to manipulate the young man was a gift that the trapper had developed over many years. Hugabone was not surprised to see Bisbee trembling.

"I guess you're more important than you look, boy. You had great influence in Harness."

Bisbee dropped to his other knee. How did this old man know such things? Maybe he was lying about the whole thing. As much as the old trapper disgusted him, he could not ignore what he had heard. If Hugabone was right, his family was suffering. Returning now might save his son from death. Did he really want to see Harness destroyed?

Hugabone smiled.

"I've been sent to bring you back. I have a letter, signed by all the Elders, stating their desire for your return and the forgiveness they will extend. It's not too late, Bisbee."

"How can I know these things are true? A man who enjoys the suffering of an innocent animal could easily lie. You have my picture, but do you have a picture of my son?"

The sun broke from behind a cloud and cast light on the old trapper. Bisbee looked into his face, in an attempt to catch some hint to his character. The old man's speech had moved from "backwoods" to that of a courtroom attorney. The silence between them was deafening.

The pull to go back to Harness was stronger than he wanted to admit. He could always return to Charis once he saw all was well. He never realized that he had so much influence in Harness.

An impatient look crept across Hugabone's face. Realizing that he was losing his "catch," the trapper decided to press the matter.

"Listen to reason. If you continue in Charis, you'll lose everything and everyone you love. You don't even know what this land holds for you. Don't you miss Avonlea? Don't you want to save your son? Come on, you're halfway across anyway."

Hugabone smiled and held his hand out. A moment earlier Bisbee had been repulsed by this man, but now he began to look at Hugabone as a friend, as someone he could possibly trust.

As if in a dream, Bisbee watched his feet begin walking back toward Harness. Suddenly, a splashing sound from under the bridge startled Bisbee. Charlie had left his hiding place and was swimming in the direction of Hugabone. As he passed by the trapper, the muskrat thrashed the water with all his might. Hugabone hurdled his body into the stream in an attempt to catch Charlie. Bisbee was frozen in his steps as he watched the scene unfold. The old trapper emerged from the water empty handed, blood flowing from his forehead. Hugabone slung his wet hair back, as he bent over to retrieve his hat from the water.

Charlie had provided the diversion that Bisbee needed. Turning around, the Traveler walked back over the bridge in the direction of Charis.

Hugabone called out to Bisbee in one last attempt to win him back to Harness, but the Traveler had learned his lesson.

"Go on, old man. I don't believe your lies. Even if it were all true, returning to Harness won't solve anything."

"You haven't heard the last from me. I'll be back. You caused me to lose two muskrats today. You'll be sorry you entered Charis."

The old trapper turned and stomped down the creek bank. Bisbee had never met anyone like Hezzy Hugabone, and he hoped that he had seen the last of him.

As he stood on the bank, Bisbee felt deeply disappointed in himself. A trip back to Harness would serve no one but himself, and as a result, he had almost followed Hugabone's counsel. He had believed that his love for Marnin was stronger than his love for himself, but apparently, he was wrong.

Bisbee stared into the creek for what seemed like forever. Finally having regained his composure, he looked upstream and wondered what had become of his little friend. Bisbee realized that Charlie had emerged from under the bridge for the purpose of distracting Hugabone, and in doing so, had risked his life. He would not blame himself if he'd seen the last of Charlie.

Bisbee stepped carefully away from the bridge and made his way down the embankment. After taking his shoes and socks off, Bisbee sat down and slipped his ankle into the cool stream.

As the water flowed over his feet, Bisbee thought about the Elders of Harness. They were such respected men, and yet they opposed this good land. Why would they choose to lead others to live in a land of defeat? They had been waging war against the Beasts for years, always with the same disastrous results. Were the reports of the rebellion true? Bisbee needed answers, and he knew who could help him. Stepping into the cool water, he turned upstream and set out to find Charlie.

The creek twisted back and forth through soft meadows. Bisbee spotted muskrat holes all along the banks, but there was no sign of Charlie. A woodchuck peered out from his hole in the distant field as a soft rain began to fall. It was a cooling sort of rain, gently kissing Bisbee's hot and tired face. The cold water of the stream felt good to his swollen ankle.

As he continued his journey upstream, the raindrops began to increase in size and intensity. The soft rain became a downpour. Knee deep in the flowing stream, Bisbee looked into the dark clouds overhead and began to laugh. In the midst of opposition, confusion and apprehension, he had never felt more alive.

This journey was like nothing he had ever expected. Instead of struggling to advance, he was being lead by a muskrat. Rather than following a well, thought out plan, he was at the mercy of curious cows and winking dragonflies. Sparrows were his warning system. In the place of a brass band and a welcoming committee, he got Hugabone. Bisbee had thought Charis would give him quick answers, but instead he saw he had much to learn. The answers he sought would be slow in coming. The land refused to yield her truth in a day.

As quickly as the downpour started, it ended. The dark clouds passed away quickly and were replaced with bright sunshine. Bisbee held his head back, closed his eyes, and allowed the sun to warm his face. When he finally opened his eyes, he saw Charlie sitting on top of an old broken dam, talking to Marnin. Even from a distance, Bisbee could see the love they shared, as they talked and laughed together. As Bisbee approached, Marnin bid farewell to Charlie and walked away. He had hoped to talk to both of them, but for some reason the Master wanted this to be a private conversation between Bisbee and his Guide.

"Enjoy the rain?" asked Charlie.

With his feet dangling from the wall, the muskrat looked down at Bisbee, and smiled.

"I forgive you for the 'slimy little rodent' comment. Now climb up and join me."

Bisbee refused to return the muskrat's smile, choosing instead to keep his eyes fixed on Charlie.

"I have some questions."

"I'm sure you do. Come sit with me; I want you to see something." Bisbee climbed up on the old dam and sat down next to Charlie on the rocky ledge.

"Look downstream. What do you see?"

Bisbee was perplexed.

"A stream," he finally responded.

Charlie said nothing, which gave Bisbee the feeling he had offered a shallow answer to a deeper question.

"Is that all?" Charlie asked.

The muskrat's eyes looked intently across the landscape. Bisbee expanded his observation.

"I see trees and grass and ..." Bisbee was confused. Whatever his little friend was trying to show him was obviously more than he was seeing. As they sat quietly on the old dam, Bisbee realized Charlie was not going to give him the answer.

He looked again at the scene before him and relaxed his mind. The stream seemed to sing as it passed over smooth rocks, meandering its way to an unknown destination. Bisbee watched as a school of brook trout swam past, occasionally coming to the surface to prey on water striders.

A flock of geese flew overhead, honking commands to each other. Bisbee followed their flight as they passed over maple trees swaying in the breeze. In the distant fields, a mother cow was welcoming her newborn calf with loud bellowing. Suddenly, a thought flashed into Bisbee's mind.

"Life. I see life."

A smile broke out on Charlie's face.

"Exactly. And do you know what we are sitting on?"

"An old dam?"

"There's hope for you yet, my friend."

Bisbee had begun to enjoy his new friend's playfulness. He was coming to understand Charlie's value as a guide.

"Bisbee, the Master works according to the principle of life. All of Charis flourishes from a common source: the life Marnin has placed within it. Hugabone's ancestors built this dam years ago in an attempt to regulate life, to use it for their own purposes."

"Wasn't that a good thing?"

"No! They almost destroyed this valley."

"What happened?"

"Marnin sent a flood, and the dam couldn't hold it back. This broken dam remains as a reminder that man must never tamper with the ways of Marnin."

Broken Dam

Charlie continued.

"When the people who built this dam saw what Marnin had done, rather than embrace him as the source of life, they fled. They settled in a new land, south of Charis, a land they named Harness. To this day, Harness is populated with their descendants."

Sitting in silence, Bisbee's mind worked furiously in an attempt to connect the dots.

"So that's why Charis is seen as a dangerous land, a valley forbidden by the Elders."

Charlie nodded.

"They still speak of Marnin as being over their land, but he is honored in name only. Sadly, they choose to live in a land where they battle the Beasts in their own ways, rather than accept the freedom of Charis. The Elders decided to send men like Hugabone back to the borders of this land to discourage anyone from crossing over into Charis. These 'sent ones,' live off the land as trappers and hunters."

Bisbee was being flooded with new information. The dam of truth had broken, and he felt as if he was floating downstream to an unknown destination... Charlie continued.

"The Elders in Harness understand they are helpless to stop the Beasts. Their hope is that the attacks will be limited, and they will somehow salvage Harness. You see Bisbee, they love to be in control of others. They're not willing to give up their power, even in the midst of the rebellion."

"So it's true; there is a rebellion?" Bisbee's eyes wandered off across the valley.

"Yes, but Hugabone's account was filled with lies."

"He lied to me. He thought if I was discouraged, I would return to Harness," Bisbee responded.

"It's why men like Hezzy Hugabone are so important to Harness. They use guilt to manipulate the followers of Marnin by the lies that they tell. They roam the borders of Charis in order to keep others in the same bondage they themselves endure."

"Are they successful?" asked Bisbee.

"Sometimes, he almost got you to return. He has his best results with those who forget about the map and the writings. The excitement of arriving in Charis overwhelms some travelers. They forget that their ultimate destination isn't Charis: it's the Well of Chayah. Their mistake is that they stop studying the map and the writings."

Bisbee dropped his head. The map and writings had fallen on the ground at the bridge. He felt for them in his pocket.

Charlie continued.

"Those who return to Harness are more miserable than those who never left. They tasted freedom in Charis, and spit it out. They are never again happy in Harness."

"If they ever were..." added Bisbee.

The Traveler had begun to understand. Why had he not seen this before? Anything man touches, he either diminishes or destroys. It is better to leave the work of Marnin alone. It is wiser to simply receive life, rather than try to channel it by human methods or for selfish ends. He had begun to see the problem in Harness might not be the Beasts after all.

"So, what about those questions you had for me, Bisbee?"

He had forgotten all about them. The new information he had been given had turned his thoughts in new directions. Instead of thinking about Harness, he realized that he needed to concentrate on the land of Charis and the mystery *of the Well of Chayah. Bisbee was determined to learn all that he could, and the sooner, the better.*

"Slow down, Bisbee. You will learn all you need to know in Marnin's time."
Charlie had read his thoughts again.

"That's really irritating."

"What? Reading your thoughts? It's a gift from the Master, and I suggest you get used to it. It may come in handy."

Charlie hopped off the dam and headed back up the hill toward the barn. Climbing down, Bisbee raced to keep up.

Charlie glanced back at Bisbee.

"That was my sister, Pearl, you saved from Hugabone's sack, and by the way, your son is not dying; he is leading the rebellion."

As incredible as it may sound, there are those who oppose the teaching of grace. There are men who are enemies of the freedom we have in Christ, and they are more abundant than we might think.[1] Surprisingly, it is from pews and pulpits that these men arise, wagging their fingers at those who have crossed over into a life of grace. Sadly, it is the advocates of religious practice and spiritual devotion that are the first to accuse the brethren of error when passing over into a life lived by God's strength alone. There are more Hugabones than you can "shake a chain at." Like old dusty trappers, they wander the borders of grace, barking out warnings at those who would enter Charis. They offer disparaging comments, directed at those who have found freedom.

The interesting thing is they would never admit to the truth that they reject grace. The word "grace" shows up in their literature and on their church signs. They warn their followers against "wild grace," and encourage a more "balanced" approach to grace. They are quick to use the phrase "cheap grace," as if there were such a thing. Taking a page out of scripture itself, they reproduce the spirit of a Pharisee in modern garb.

Beating the drums to a century's old argument, they sound the alarm that radical grace will become nothing more than a license to sin. Paul was compelled to answer this very accusation.[2] These law-based brethren warn us that straying from the path of obedience to the commands of scripture will lead us down a road toward riotous living. Nothing could be further from the truth.

Before going any further, let's define legalism. Legalism involves asking the believer to "do" something in order to grow and be blessed. It amounts to a list of duties given as a prerequisite for the Christian's maturation and fruit-bearing. The result of legalism is bondage. The law-based believer has forgotten Paul's question to the Galatians. "Having begun in the Spirit, are you now being perfected by the flesh?"[3]

Those who teach law lay out well-designed strategies for the establishment of progress toward spiritual adulthood. From their perspective, every angle of sanctification is covered, producing a foolproof pathway to advancement in spiritual matters. Why would we set up a system of strategies for growth, when Jesus told us to simply abide?

My Uncle Leland kept an old bull named "Jug-Head" in his barn. A hayloft stood above his pen with a small hole in the floor. As kids, we would stand over the hole, tossing hay down on the massive creature. Our purpose was to irritate the fire out of Jug Head. We loved hearing him snort deeply, paw the ground, and charge the walls of his pen. It was exciting to stand over the hole and look down at him. The opening was just big enough for us to fall through, which added to our excitement. Walls and gates restrained Jug Head, giving us a false sense of control over the beast. We knew that with one small slip through the hole, we would be at Jug Head's mercy. Take the fences down and disaster would reign; however, fall through the hole, and the ferocious bull would certainly put an end to our lives.

Within every Christian is a beast called the flesh. The legalist has adopted strategies for dealing with this dilemma. According to his mindset, concentration on the commands of scripture terrifies Jug Head, maintaining a consistent prayer life quiets the bull, and staying busy in service leaves no time for him. By these measures, the beast is kept at a safe distance. But the Jug Head within us all is neither threatened nor deterred by these activities; in fact, he's right at home.

The legalist who relies on law would never say grace is not needed; but rather, it is not enough to keep you safe. Grace, in their minds, must be "balanced" with obedience to the commands of scripture. Their goal is to restrain Jug Head with strategies and methods. But does the

Bible say, "we are more than restrainers in Christ," or "we are more than conquerors in Christ?"[4]

The real problem with this approach is that the focus of our attention shifts from Christ to the methods themselves. It is what some have labeled "sin management." With a desire to contain the uncontainable, the law-based believer creates a comfortable web of activity. Legislating every aspect of the Christian life: prayer, Bible study, church attendance, etc., spiritual growth is neatly categorized. As long as the lists are diligently followed, a safe distance from the bull is maintained. Outbreaks of the beast are seen as a direct result of veering off the path of obedience.

In the same way that a familiar blanket comforts a child, "doing the list," gives Christians a sense of safety and protection. Take away our spiritual checkpoints, and we feel exposed and vulnerable. It's much more reassuring to have the church, or the preacher, simply tell us every move to make. Legalism is nothing more than a counter-balance to sin and in the end it leaves us defeated and perplexed. Rather than look to ourselves, we were meant to live by His "life," which dwells in us.[5]

Paul was well acquainted with battling those who wanted to keep believers under law. In Second Corinthians, he labeled them as ministers of death.[6] To the Christians of the Galatian region, Paul warned them to flee from those who would enslave them again in a yoke of bondage. The Galatians had been "called" to freedom.[7] By focusing on obedience, they had taken their eyes off of Christ. Nothing but slavery can result from an emphasis on obedience rather than faith.

Paul used the strongest language possible in describing the motives of these teachers. Filled with pride, and driven by lust, their goal was to control others.[8] Parading their pedigrees, they laid down qualifications for becoming spiritual. The bondage Paul rejected in favor of simply knowing Christ, they peddled. Blind to the freedom Christ had purchased, their desire was to bury others in an avalanche of commands.

If there was ever a man who had reason to be religiously proud, it was Paul. He possessed perfect national heritage, religious roots second to none, and a passion for God.[9] His devotion to the Jewish religion led him to take violent action against the Christian church.[10]

In the third chapter of his letter to the Philippians, he listed his accomplishments. Paul wrapped all those impressive achievements in a neat bundle and dropped them in the city dump when he met Christ.[11] He realized none of his lofty endeavors advanced him one iota. Lost in the magnificence of Christ, he came to view his pedigrees as nothing more than a cheap tin badge, worn by a broken down sheriff.

The joy of simply knowing Christ overwhelmed Paul. Notice carefully that serving Christ or being obedient was not his goal. It was Paul's desire to know Him and the power of His resurrected life that motivated the Apostle.[12]

Paul paid dearly for his decision to follow Jesus. He described it as suffering the loss of all things. What things did he lose? How did he suffer? Perhaps it was the loss of friends. His lifelong comrades in Judaism no doubt turned on him. Perhaps he lost the praise of man. When he abandoned his religious roots, he had no doubt lost his position in Judaism. When Paul passed by, heads turned in dismay. Smiles turned to frowns, as insults and threats became his common experience.

Rejected by friends and possibly family, he followed the path of grace. Leaving behind the applause of men, he focused his attention on one subject: Christ. By embracing God's unmerited favor, Paul trusted Christ alone to be his righteousness. He turned his back on establishing his own righteousness in favor of receiving grace. The decision Paul made (to believe in radical grace), extended itself far beyond the moment of his conversion. The man, who had been knocked to the ground on his way to Damascus, would never walk again by his own strength. After having begun in the Spirit, he refused to adopt human effort to complete the journey.

By our strength we can do nothing; by our effort we only fail. Complete victory was accomplished on the cross of Jesus. In his closing remarks to the Galatians, Paul stated, that an attempt to keep the law removes the offense of the cross.[13] It is a deathblow to human pride to declare that we can do nothing to please Him. Nothing can be added to His perfect work. Nothing! Jesus is not only the Author of our faith, He is the Finisher.[14]

Are you ready for grace to be the anthem of your life? When faith is your rallying cry, human effort will be finished. Are you ready to reject the Hugabones of religion? Steel traps leave ugly wounds.

CHAPTER 7

THE BEAST

As Bisbee walked along the creek bank, he experienced a deep sense of joy. He was glad he had chosen to stay in Charis. Only a short distance lay between the two banks, and yet the difference was enormous. On the road back to Harness, fear, doubt and failure crept over the path like a silent death; however, on Charis's banks, peace, joy, and rest filled the land like the smell of a flowering lilac.

Having made their way back to the bridge, Charlie abruptly stopped. The muskrat dropped his head, his eyes searching the ground for the right words to say. Bisbee noticed his change in mood. Storm clouds gathered overhead, hiding the sun and casting a pale darkness on the land. A cold, north wind blew against Bisbee's face as a wild dog howled in the distance. Charlie slowly raised his head and looked intently into the Sojourner's eyes.

"Bisbee, in this land you will learn things about yourself you never expected. It's a painful discovery, my friend, but it's one you have to experience alone."

Bisbee went numb.

Suddenly Charlie grew serious. "I have to go; he's coming."

The muskrat looked past Bisbee to the top of the hill where the Master was sitting. Charlie slowly nodded his head and before Bisbee could say a word, his guide slid into the water and disappeared. The Traveler turned to see Marnin walking into the woods. His back was turned to Bisbee.

Almost immediately, the ground began to shake. Bisbee looked toward the distant cornfields and saw stalks flying in the air like dry javelins. A cloud of dust covered the ground with each thunderous crash. Whatever was approaching *filled Bisbee with great fear. Running up the path to the black walnut tree, he took shelter behind its rough bark. The thunder came closer and closer.*

Walnuts dropped like hail onto Bisbee's head. Charlie had abandoned him, but what help would a muskrat be in a moment like this? Bisbee needed the Master, but He was nowhere to be found. Had Marnin brought him to Charis to watch him die?

The tremors intensified with each passing moment, lifting Bisbee off the ground. And then, silence. Well almost...

Bisbee heard deep breathing, like a train when it is starting down the tracks. A sickening odor filled the air, choking him. Green with nausea, he doubled over. Fearful of being discovered, Bisbee held back the urge to vomit. Sweat, pouring down his face, he hugged the back of the walnut tree as if his life depended on it.

The breathing slowly subsided. He could wait no longer; he had to see what was on the other side. With great timidity he turned, still hugging the tree. Pushing his face up against the bark, he worked his way around the trunk. The breathing stopped. Stepping out into the open, Bisbee faced his greatest fear.

Shocked to the core, Bisbee stood frozen in time. Standing before him was one of the Beasts of Harness. Years of dark curiosity were swept away in a moment as the creature lifted its head.

"An elephant...?" Bisbee whispered.

The Beast

The smell of sour molasses overwhelmed Bisbee's senses. He had smelled it before. The tusks of the elephant were cracked and yellowed with age. The Beast's eyes ran with thick yellow mucus from some sort of infection. Horse flies gathered around his head to drink of the foul discharge. They were the same flies that had tormented the people of Harness. Looking back into the eyes of the elephant, Bisbee gasped. Buried deeply in the Beast's dark pupils, Bisbee saw a clear reflection of himself. Stumbling backwards he felt disoriented.

As the Beast stepped toward him, Bisbee felt as if they knew each other. He sensed an awkward attachment to the Beast, as if this was his elephant. Bisbee had always thought of the creatures as something separate from him, but now the connection he felt was undeniable. He suddenly realized this was the very Beast he had battled long ago in Harness. As the dust continued to settled, Bisbee recalled a night back in Harness, long ago.

Bisbee was returning home from a night of hunting when he spotted the shadow of a Beast grazing in a field. Moving slowly through the tall grass, he positioned himself behind the creature. Running at full sprint, Bisbee attempted to thrust his spear into its leathery hide. Swinging his spear wildly, Bisbee cut the creature's left ear, causing the Beast to thrash in the thicket so violently that Bisbee backed away in fear. He attempted to identify the creature, but before he could he was knocked to the ground. He never forgot that night. There was no question in his mind that the Beast before him was the same one he had battled on that night long ago.

As the dust settled around the elephant before him, so did the memory. Something was clinging to the Beast. Mounted just behind the elephant's head was the hideous creature he had seen in Coopers Cave. Hidden behind its massive ears, the figure was so thin and pale he could be easily overlooked. Riding comfortably on the massive animal, the elephant and rider were in full concert. Sickened, he looked away from the rider, choosing to refocus his attention on the Beast.

Preparing for battle, Bisbee felt for his knife. Realizing he had left it behind in Harness, he found a broken branch lying next to the walnut tree. Pawing the ground, the elephant prepared to charge. Lifting his trunk, he issued a battle cry, knocking Bisbee to the ground. Feeling something tear into his flesh, he looked down to see blood flowing from his right arm. A strand of rusty barbwire hidden in the grass had ripped into his forearm.

Pulling the wire from the grassy bank, Bisbee raised it high above his head and turned to face the Beast. The elephant lowered its head, as the rider threw his head high in the air, letting out a sickening cry. Adrenaline surged through Bisbee's veins, heightening his senses. This elephant was his to kill and today he would not fail.

Suddenly, everything changed. Without warning and for no apparent reason, the Traveler hesitated. Dropping his head, he threw the wire back into the grass. What high level of insanity would make him think a rusty piece of wire could bring down his foe? He had used all the weapons of Harness, and none of them had been effective. Why would today be any different? Bisbee looked around the countryside. He was in Charis now and this place was different.

Blood dripping from his fingertips, Bisbee slowly turned and walked away. The elephant continued bellowing, but he refused to turn back. Bisbee had yet to learn the secrets of Charis, but he was determined never again to fight the Beast using the old and tired methods of Harness.

Sitting down next to the walnut tree, Bisbee was exhausted. Suddenly, he saw something out of the corner of his eye. It was Charlie, sitting on the dam, and from his vantage point, the muskrat had apparently witnessed the entire scene. A surprising emotion crept into Bisbee. He felt shame. A connection to the Beast was something he had not expected… and now Charlie knew. Bisbee quickly looked away from his friend.

Turning toward the bridge, he saw movement under the Willow Tree. Marnin was sitting on the east bank of Living Stream. How long had he been there? Had he seen Bisbee's shameful display on the battlefield? Did he know of the personal connection the Traveler had with the elephant? There was only one way to know for sure.

Lifting his weary head, he forced himself to look into Marnin's eyes. Instantly, Bisbee knew. His proud heart was torn beyond recognition, and the shame Bisbee felt in that moment was overwhelming. The Master had probably known all along.

Feeling as though a ton of bricks had landed on his chest, he collapsed under its load. Falling to the ground, Bisbee wept uncontrollably. He knew he was responsible for his own misery and the heartache of countless others. But most of all, he had hurt Marnin. Bisbee had repaid the purest love he had ever known by allowing the Beast to wreak havoc in his life. He felt as if a knife had punctured his heart, and all he wanted to do was push it in further.

Bisbee finally lifted his head and looked back down to the stream. There sat the Master, quietly watching. How could Marnin love him now? Looking back down, he stared into a pile of cracked walnuts surrounding him. Waiting for what seemed like forever, he looked back toward the bridge, hoping Marnin would not be there. Still sitting under the willow, the Master had not moved. He wanted to shout to the Master to go away, but the words would not come.

Through tear-filled eyes, Bisbee looked back toward the field of conflict. The Beast and its rider were returning to the shadows from which they came. A twisted smile spread across the face of the rider. Throwing the map and writings into the field, the Traveler fell to the ground and buried his face in the dirt.

Bisbee beat his fist into the pile of cracked, fallen walnuts, until his hand bled. He longed for a hiding place where no one could ever find him. A cave would work just fine.

There is an elephant in the room. He is big and smelly. No one wants to talk about him, but he is definitely "in the room". He has ruined many a church social, divided fellowships, and in extreme cases even caused physical death. This uncontrollable beast has ruined marriages, ended relationships, and caused heartache beyond description. The pesky pachyderm is the best-kept secret in the church.

In order to reveal the elephant, we must first understand God's internal work within us. When a man comes to Christ, the very nature of God enters.[1] The sin nature that used to dominate the man, becomes what the Bible calls the "old man." The presence of the "new man" (Christ living in him) has presented us with the dilemma of this "old man." Paul preached his own funeral service in Romans chapter six, when he declared that the "old man" had been crucified with Christ.[2] Does this mean that sin has been eradicated? No, of course not! This principle of sin, still residing in the believer, is more than an old recording from the past: it is an ever-present reality, and it is as powerful as it has ever been.

The "new man" in Christ still has within him something called "flesh."[3] Its origin and why God chooses to allow it to remain is a mystery. What is not a mystery is the undeniable power that the flesh still holds. The elephant of "self-life" is alive and well and it will not be defeated by any amount of effort.[4] This beast will not be restrained by attempts to repress it, nor will it wander off as a result of our busy activities as Christians.

To be clear, the flesh in this context is not the physical stuff hanging from our skeletons. God created our skin, our physical being, and it is good. The elephant of flesh is a highly visible, invisible, presence within that we become acutely aware of when we begin growing in grace. It dwells in our bodies, but it is separate from our physical being. Sin may use our physical members but it remains something other. We know that our bodies can be used for good because the Scripture declares God's desire to use them for His glory.[5] Our physical bodies are neutral entities in the scheme of things. Sin may use our physical members, but God created us and He declares our bodies to be good, based on His creation. It is important that these things are clearly differentiated in our minds.

It is also vital to understand that when the Bible speaks of "sin," (the singular form), it is viewed as a principle within us. When "sins" (the plural form) are mentioned it is the act of sinning that is in view.

Think about how a factory operates. It produces a product but at the same time it is separate from it's product.

God has not only provided forgiveness for our sins, but He has also given us a remedy for the "factory" that produces the sins. God has provided a source of victory, but it is of great importance that we first recognize and acknowledge the true nature of the beast.

The elephant does his best work under the cover of darkness. We provide it with the cover needed to establish its base of operation within us. We should be actively repelling the darkness of this beast, but instead we make a thousand excuses for its presence. If we are providing its cover, how can we hope to be free of its tyranny? In addition to this perplexing scenario, the flesh is an intangible entity. How can we hunt and kill an animal that we cannot see, touch, taste, or smell?

To discover the true source of our sinful behavior and to know the depths of our carnality, we must seek the answer in a place other than ourselves. Our own hearts will lead us astray. Without realizing it, we will water down our true condition until we embrace remedies, which ultimately fall short of deliverance. Our inability to come to terms with the depth of sin within us is the reason we adopt shallow methods to fix the unfixable.

The only reliable source is the Bible. Only God, who created us and fully understands our plight, can accurately expose the corruption of the flesh. God has declared our true condition, and He has done so for a very specific purpose.

The prophet Jeremiah clearly states that our hearts are so "desperately wicked," that we do not even have the capacity to discover the depths of depravity.[6] The Hebrew word he uses for "desperate," is a word meaning to be "incurably sick," with the idea of the heart being frail and feeble. In an eye-opening indictment, Isaiah declares that our righteous acts are as unclean things, "filthy rags" in the courts of heaven.[7]

Suppose, for a moment, that we could ask our hearts the source of all our troubles. If we asked a liar to tell us the truth, what should we expect to hear? If we invited a thief to stay at our house while on vacation, what do you think we would find upon returning? In the same way a liar will not be truthful, and a thief cannot be trusted, neither can the heart be expected to admit its own evil. Human reasoning simply cannot be trusted in these matters.

At the moment of conversion, we receive the Divine nature, but the Flesh remains unaltered. This explains how we can still think, say and do the same sinful things. Flesh remains flesh. God does not spiritualize the flesh when we become believers.

Paul described the battle between the Flesh and Spirit as a great conflict.[8] The word he used, to explain their relationship, was "contrary," which means to be completely opposite.

Jesus told Nicodemis, "that which is flesh is flesh."[9] In fact, it is *because* He lives in us, that we now have the ability to see the true wickedness of the flesh. The Holy Spirit is like a bright light, shining within us, exposing our carnality, and yet at the same time revealing His holiness.

At this juncture, you might be tempted to retreat, but the reality of His presence will console you in this tough moment of revelation. In truth, if you continue reading this book, it shows that have a real hunger for answers.

It is only when you reach the end of your rope that God begins to pull you onto a safe ledge. Oswald Chambers once said, "According to the Bible, God is only manifested at the last point; when a man is driven by personal experience to the last limit, he is apt to meet God."[10]

The seventh chapter of the book of Romans was written from the perspective of a saved man attempting to free himself from the power of sin. The Apostle Paul's conclusion at the end of this chapter was a shocking discovery. After a long struggle to restrain evil and perform righteousness, he cried out in despair, "in my flesh dwells no good thing."[11] This was a great moment of revelation for Paul.

Allow the phrase, "no good thing," to resonate. Spun wildly by the miserable-go-round of obedience to the law, he finally jumped off. The law provided plenty of direction but absolutely no power to be obedient to its endless demands. This revelation dawned on Paul only after a great struggle had taken place within his soul.[12]

Our hope of someday conquering sin by our spiritual disciplines and self-effort dies a slow death. We struggle for years, using different methods in an attempt to overcome the power of sin in our lives, with

little or no success. Stay on the merry-go-round long enough and you
will turn green. Viewing the same miserable landscape of law, year after
year, causes one to reel with dizziness. Nearing the end of our striving
we begin to reach out for real answers.

The counsel we receive in these times of distress is not always
helpful. You may have quietly raised your hand in the assembly of
the saints, or confided in a brother or sister in Christ that you were
struggling with sin, only to be quickly ushered off to a counseling room
and handed a notepad of spiritual prescriptions. A helpful book might be
offered which includes a carefully thought-out program sure to defeat
those pesky flesh patterns. Perhaps you were sent home with countless
remedies to fix your "sinful" condition.

It may have been suggested you were never saved in the first place,
since, they say, no true believer would be struggling with ongoing
sin issues. You were given assurances all would be well if you just
memorized a few key verses from the Bible; however, the more effort
you exerted, the further you were from victory.

The treadmill of ceaseless activity can go on for years. In time, you
may stop asking the uncomfortable questions that no one seems able to
answer. You might conclude that struggling is just a normal experience.
You can come to the false conclusion that the best you can hope for is
to manage the embarrassing elephant without getting too much mess
on your shoes.

When God confronted Adam concerning his sin, a pattern began
that continues to this day. When asked whether he had sinned with
the forbidden fruit, Adam back-peddled, pointed his finger at Eve, and
ultimately blamed God.[13] Adam refused to accept responsibility for his
rebellion. Caught red-handed, he attempted to cover for his sin. He did
what mankind has been doing ever since. He did what Christians still
do. Adam denied the reality of his sinful act, which proceeded from a
rebellious heart. The problem is not our sinful acts; but our rebellious
heart.

The wickedness dwelling in us is unredeemable, unalterable, and
beyond hope of change. Our sins were forgiven but our flesh was not.
It remains in a state of constant rebellion.[14] The elephant is in the room,
and until we agree with God and shine the bright light of Scripture

on the beast, he will continue to wreak havoc. Are you ready to stop pretending that the elephant does not exist?

It is crucial that we fully embrace God's estimation of our sinful flesh. Sin hides behind a thousand masks. It is a big pill to swallow, but until the pill goes down, you will progress no further. Get a big glass of water; you're going to need it.

CHAPTER 8

THE MAGAN

Bisbee sat at the base of the walnut tree for what seemed like forever. Dazed and confused, he struggled to make sense of all he had just experienced. The memory of Marnin sitting under the willow, looking at him with loving acceptance, was like a hound that would not wander off. As many bones as Bisbee threw into the field, the dog would not leave. The vision of Marnin's loving face was relentless. Lost in despair and buried in hopelessness, his only desire was to be left alone with his broken heart. He felt as if he would never be free from the Beast. An indestructible foe was threatening the destruction of his people. Why go on?

For reasons unknown, the Traveler decided to attempt to climb out of his lethargy. As he struggled to get up, Bisbee's knee struck an exposed root, sending lightning bolts of pain coursing through his body. Looking down at the blood, now pulsating from his kneecap, Bisbee reared his head back and laughed. The pain of being cut open was a relief to Bisbee; for a moment he could be numb, displaced from the misery he had just experienced. Bisbee realized how ill prepared he had been to learn of his attachment to the Beast. Charis had revealed the ugly truth, and a part of him wished he had never crossed the bridge. It would have been better to stay in Harness and remain ignorant.

Perched high in the willow tree, the old crow screamed again.

"Go back, go back!"

He knew that returning to Harness was no longer a possibility. Having seen the elephant, he could no longer face the people he loved. The only news he could send back was a report of misery. Harness was not ready to know the depth of the danger they faced.

The crow in the willow continued her relentless attack on the Traveler's nerves.

"Go back! Go back, you fool!"

Picking up a stone, Bisbee located the bird hidden in the willow branches. He hesitated, and instead, tossed the rock into a nearby field. He decided to let the black bird have her day. Content to sit among the fallen walnuts in defeat, Bisbee was not concerned about his next move.

Suddenly he heard a splashing sound from the creek bank. Charlie was walking toward him with a pleasant smile. A small fish wiggled hopelessly in the little muskrat's claws. Charlie was in a jovial mood. He had caught a fish, which was a rare feat for a muskrat. Sitting down next to Bisbee, he began devouring his prey. After a long silence, broken only by the crunching of tiny fish bones, Bisbee spoke.

"It was an elephant, Charlie."

"Yes, I know."

"It was my elephant."

"I know. Everyone has one."

This had not been the first time that Charlie sat beside a Traveler in turmoil. The quiet and persistent shock of their connection to the Beast was always difficult for Charlie to watch, but he had learned over time not to lessen the pain of this necessary wound. As difficult as it was for the little muskrat, Charlie kept his mouth shut.

"Tell me about the elephant rider."

Charlie turned away.

"Marnin prefers for you to know as little as possible about him."

"What's his name?"

"I'm not supposed to tell you."

Bisbee stared in Charlie's direction until the muskrat could take it no longer.

"Spit Yak. His name is Spit Yak. He was assigned to you by the enemy the day you decided to follow Marnin."

"What do you mean he was assigned to me by the Enemy?"

Charlie had already said too much. Turning away from Bisbee, he walked over to the barbwire fence.

As Bisbee stared into the open field, a chill ran down his spine. He felt eerie, as if he had been placed in one of those unearthly stories that he had often read to his children. Who was this revolting creature named Spit Yak, and what was he doing riding the elephant? Had Spit Yak always been present, or did he only occasionally ride the Beast? Bisbee stood up and joined the muskrat at the fence. In a somber tone, Bisbee spoke.

"Charlie, did the elephant follow me across the bridge? Did I bring him into Charis?"

Charlie wasn't listening. He regretted telling Bisbee about the elephant rider and was searching for an explanation he could give Marnin. The crow screamed again.

"Go back. Go back!"

Charlie looked up.

"Ignore the old crow. It's all she ever says. They're not very smart, you know."

The muskrat had regained his composure.

"You're a mess Bisbee. Come down to the creek and wash yourself off."

"You could have warned me," Bisbee protested.

"No amount of warning would have prepared you for the moment. Besides, a good guide knows when to show up and when to disappear. Bisbee, it's something you had to face alone."

"Don't you understand? The people of Harness are depending on me to bring back answers. My family and friends are facing certain disaster. Sending back good news will aid in the rebellion. It will stall without my help. The people of Harness are clueless as to the danger of these Beasts. I'm here in Charis to find answers. Charlie, I'm the only hope they have!"

"Only hope?"

"That's right."

"Everyone's depending on you?"

"I thought I was quite clear."

Charlie looked amused.

"What's so funny, little fellow?"

"You are. Do you really think it all depends on you? I see a lot of pride in you, Bisbee."

The Traveler flashed with anger. What right did Charlie have to talk to him like that? He decided he did not like this little rodent after all.

"It's not pride; I care about my people."

Charlie smiled as Bisbee washed off his face.

"Bisbee, your experience seeing the Beast was not intended to make you believe that you should rescue the people of Harness."

Bisbee looked offended. This journey was about the deliverance of his people. What other possible reason could there be?

The cows had migrated down to the lower pasture and were crowding the fence to watch and listen to the exchange. Bisbee hated their eyes. Chewing their cud, they seemed to enjoy his pain.

"What if there is something more important than Harness at stake?" Charlie asked.

"What could be more important than rescuing my friends and family? What do you mean?"

Charlie smiled sympathetically. He knew Bisbee was held back by what he confidently "knew," and blinded by his "clear" vision. It would require a great deal of patience on the part of the muskrat before Bisbee's proud heart would understand. A soft wind began to blow against the Traveler's face.

"I think the Master can deliver the people of Harness without your help," the muskrat finally replied.

"Bisbee, the sooner you realize this whole journey isn't about you rescuing others, the quicker we'll get to our destination."

"So let me get this straight. What I just experienced has nothing to do with what's going on in Harness? Sounds like I'm wasting my time. Maybe you're wasting my time!"

Bisbee was obviously agitated. Charlie's face tightened.

"We can go no further until you understand why you're here. You're the one wasting time."

Turning to walk away, Charlie began whistling.

"Hey, where are you going?" Bisbee protested. "I need your help."

Bisbee stood helpless, left alone on a path going nowhere. He wished he had not spoken to Charlie in such a rough manner. The company of a muskrat was preferable to the loneliness he was now experiencing. Would Charlie return, if he shouted an apology? The deafening sound of a prison cell door closing in on him was interrupted by the sound of soft footsteps behind him.

"Bisbee."

The Traveler knew who it was before ever turning around. It was the last voice he wanted to hear, and yet, he was strangely relieved to hear it. It was music to his ears and sandpaper to his soul all at the same time. Turning to face the Master, he fell to his knees, refusing to look up. Bisbee deeply desired to look into Marnin's eyes, but his heart was filled with fear and shame.

He now knew he was tied to the Beast, and the shock was multiplied a thousand times in the presence of Marnin. The thickness of silence was filling Bisbee's lungs as every passing moment brought a deeper sense of shame. If Marnin did not walk away soon, Bisbee felt as if he would surely die. How could the Master still love him after knowing the pain he had caused? How could he remain steadfast in the midst of Bisbee's unfaithfulness to him?

Bisbee kept his head down, hoping the Master would turn and walk away, but all he heard was the babbling of the creek. If there was ever a time for Marnin to abandon him, it would be now.

"Bisbee, lift your eyes."

Slowly raising his head, his eyes refused to climb higher than Marnin's chest. Time slowed to a crawl. Locked in his prison of humiliation, he wanted to turn and run, but something held him there. It was as if warm cords were drawing him in.

"Bisbee, look into my eyes." Slowly, he raised his head and looked into Marnin's eyes.

The next few moments seemed like a dream to Bisbee. Never before had he experienced such intense love. Flowing from the Masters eyes were a thousand messages of compassion without a spoken word. How could Marnin still love him? Bisbee suddenly turned away, sickened at the thought that he had disappointed such amazing love.

"Don't turn away! I have been eagerly awaiting this moment."

Bisbee was perplexed. Had he heard the Master right? He had been waiting for what moment? The moment all his hopes would come crashing down into a pile of useless rubble? The moment he realized he was responsible for his Beast?

"My friend…You don't understand, do you?"

Marnin reached out and touched Bisbee's arm. Surprised, the Master still called him friend, he looked again into his eyes. Charlie had rejoined them and was sitting at the base of a mulberry bush.

"No, I don't," Bisbee finally replied.

"Finally we're getting somewhere. The Traveler has finally admitted he didn't understand something," Charlie exclaimed.

"Let me handle this, my little friend," said the Master.

"My apologies."

"No apology necessary." Marnin and Charlie shared a smile as the Master turned His attention back toward Bisbee.

"You need to understand you are of little use in Charis until you realize you are of no use in Charis."

Bursting into laughter, the muskrat clutched his stomach and fell over into the soft clover.

"Forgive him, Bisbee. He always gets tickled at that line."

"I see no humor in it. It doesn't even make sense," Bisbee replied.

"Listen carefully Bisbee, until you abandon all hope in your abilities to conquer your elephant, you will continue to battle him on your own terms and in your own way. Every time you will lose."

Charlie had collected himself and was looking intently into Bisbee's eyes. The Master continued.

"You will struggle and fail until you realize you are no match for him."

The wheels began to turn in Bisbee's mind.

"Isn't this journey supposed to be a struggle, a battle plan of some kind? I need to send a new strategy back to Harness."

"No."

Bisbee protested.

"All of life is a struggle. If we don't fight, how will we ever be free? We need new weapons of some sort and a plan of action."

The Master leaned forward placing his hand on the side of Bisbee's face. Marnin spoke softly and yet with firmness.

"I will not argue this point with you. There will be no victory until you take your hands off of the elephant. The mystery of the Well of Chayah will not yield its treasure to a heart that battles. You are blinded by what you see and unable to learn because you 'know so much.' It is your pride, Bisbee, that keeps you in this place of failure."

Marnin began walking away when suddenly he stopped and turned back toward Bisbee.

"As for the rider, Charlie should not have told you his name; it's unimportant."

Marnin glanced sternly in Charlie's direction, but the muskrat was looking off into a distant field.

"When the elephant goes, the rider goes with him. The key, Bisbee, is the elephant." Having spoken his last word on the subject, Marnin turned and walked up Ascending Hill.

Bisbee stood in silence. The Master's words were beginning to penetrate his soul. It was pride that had kept him in bondage all those years in Harness. It wasn't the Elders or the Beasts that had brought failure and defeat; it was himself. Charlie walked over to where he was standing. The muskrat resisted the temptation to add anything to Marnin's counsel. He knew it was a huge pill to swallow.

"Pride?"

Bisbee could see it now. It was as if a window sash had been suddenly thrown open, and all he could see was his pride, a cloud of dust hanging heavily in the sunlight.

He turned to his guide.

"What does he expect from me?"

"Nothing," replied Charlie.

"Bisbee, he wants you to know that the elephant is too big for you."

Bisbee put his head down and began to weep. Confessing his blindness and ignorance, he finally surrendered to the wisdom of the Master. The long, silent battle he had waged was over. He looked up into the bright blue sky and saw a red-breasted robin in flight. On her wings, she carried away Bisbee's struggle. He finally saw he was no match for the elephant, and the release he experienced was beyond description.

In that moment, Bisbee felt unspeakable freedom. A thousand burdens lifted their wings and flew from the Traveler's soul. Bisbee's heart was as light as a feather.

Charlie sat patiently, allowing him time to experience the joy of release. The muskrat had seen it a thousand times. He had watched as travelers laid down the struggle, finally understanding their complete uselessness in defeating their elephants. It was always an exciting moment for the muskrat, filling him with wonder. Charlie looked up the hill at the Master in calm adoration. He loved Marnin's patience and willingness to wait through years of battling until his followers abandoned their efforts. This was the moment of the Traveler's "Magan."

An old barn owl let out a deafening screech, jarring Bisbee back to the present. He glanced at Charlie.

"You're still here? I thought you'd be hunting crawfish."

Smiling at Bisbee, Charlie decided to ignore the mild poke.

"We've got a long way to go my friend, and this is only the beginning,"
Charlie replied. The muskrat fixed his eyes toward the barnyard.

"I'm ready Charlie, but I do have one question."

"Go ahead."

The muskrat had picked up a black walnut and was attempting to crack its shell.

"Why didn't I recognize the elephant in Harness?"

Charlie looked up.

"They never felt threatened in Harness. The Land of Charis terrifies them."

It is a great discovery when we realize that life is too big for us. The power of the flesh is beyond our ability to comprehend, much less conquer. Our attempt to conquer sin in our lives is as futile as bringing a stick to a gunfight. We always end up being shot full of holes.

Until we come to the end of ourselves and to the end of our freedom-struggle, our eyes cannot be opened to the power of the flesh. We are stubborn creatures. We run into the brick wall of failure a thousand times. Finally, bloodied and toothless, we raise the white flag of surrender. Why does it take so long?

The enticing bait of human achievement is too alluring. It is possible to be in the trap of effort for a long time. The trap finally springs when sin is seen as a thing too powerful for us. The release will never come until the trap of human effort snaps shut. It is hard to turn away from the eyes of the cobra. We are mesmerized by the thought that the next strategy will work. Spiritual advancement is not possible by human effort; the beautiful thing is, He does not expect it to be.[1]

To drop this burden of self-imposed disciplines is to be moved to a place of complete dependence on the Lord. This resembles a nervous breakdown but in a spiritual context. Paul revealed this when he wrote, "Not I, but Christ."[2] (Notice the order: first we must learn, "Not I," and then we are ready to embrace, "but Christ.")

Released from preoccupation with self, the freedom-experience of self-forgetfulness is liberating. How important we thought we were... and suddenly we are not. Throwing our spiritual thermometers in the trash, the game of whether we are "hot or cold," is over. As we begin to experience the grace and love of Christ, (apart from our performance), we are reintroduced to the simplicity of Christ. No longer do we trust ourselves.[3]

The responsibility of our walk with Christ has been placed firmly on Him. He not only forgives our sins; He also assumes the great task of living His life through us. His life in us is the great motivating factor. Christ's power, not ours, fulfills the commands of scripture. He does not help us to be obedient; He is our obedience.[4]

Do you remember the joy of being forgiven when you first came to Christ? No demands or expectations were required of you. Salvation was clear, it was simple, and it was finished. When did it get complicated?

It may have started when a well-meaning brother or sister in Christ gave you a list of duties to perform. Maybe every time you got "on fire for Jesus," the bucket brigade showed up. Years of thankless service can gut spiritual fervor. Just the vicious cycle of church life can wear the best Christian down. Maybe you blame God for the blows of life that came after you gave your heart to Jesus. Overthinking the simple, the analytical mind thinks thoughts of self-vindication to the point of strangling the life of Jesus to death. Perhaps it began with the thought that you needed to serve Him for all He had done for you. What has stolen your joy? Burdened with whatever has weighed you down, your clear streams of joy turned murky. What is desperately needed is that we look away from ourselves to the only One that can deliver us. Christ alone is to be our life and sanctification.

Have you ever been disappointed with yourself? The source of disappointment is unrealized expectations. Expect nothing from yourself and you can never be disappointed. If we expect, even with His help, to be able to live for Christ, then we set ourselves up for failure. If we believe we can please the Lord through our disciplines and devotion, our failure to keep our eyes on Him brings our downfall.

Nowhere in the Bible are we told to evaluate our walk with Christ. We are encouraged to make sure we are, "in the faith,"[5] but never are we prodded to judge our progress or that of anyone else. We can only look at one thing at a time. If we place our eyes on ourselves, at that moment we have taken our eyes off of Christ. We grow by "looking unto Jesus," who is the Author and Finisher of our faith.[6]

When we discover He has no expectations of us, we relax. We begin to understand our position in the equation: absent. As Paul asked, "Where is boasting; it is excluded."[7] The commands of scripture are not directed toward us, but to His Life in us. He does all.

I had a college professor who became frustrated on the first day of class. His students were asking questions concerning grading methods for the course, and he finally stopped the inquiries with this statement.

"Everyone in the class has an A; now relax and let's learn."

It was one of the best courses I ever took. With no pressure, we were relaxed and encouraged to learn. It is from the position of rest that His life is communicated to us. When Jesus saved us, we were given His righteousness.[8] In that righteousness we are to confidently walk. His righteousness makes us a perfect ten. Our standing before the Father never changes.[9] From resting, we walk, while walking we stand. We may stumble and fall, but nothing changes our perfect position before the Father. We can always rest in that. The Lord may discipline us because He is our Father, but that does not change the fact that when He looks at us, He sees Jesus. This truth gives stability to the whole process of growth.

Jesus made it simple when He said, "Come unto Me."[10] If you think of it, isn't that the last thing we do? We read the latest book, encouraging some new method for spiritual growth. We are careful to check off every item on the list that men give us. The idea of simply "coming to Jesus," seems, well... too simple.

If you carefully read the invitation of Jesus to come unto Him, you will find that the question is posed to those who are worn-out. If you still have strength, keep battling. You are not ready yet. It is only those who are weary that find themselves in the place of rest. He promised His yoke to the exhausted. He will not help us as long as we continue to battle sin in our own strength.

Have you ever heard a believer bemoan the difficulty of the Christian life, struggling under the weight of his "cross"? The New

Testament teaches no such thing! Jesus stated that His yoke was easy and His burden was light. This does not mean that difficult trials will not come our way or that we won't suffer. What it does mean is that we should rest in Him, and lightness in the midst of heaviness is an evidence of His presence.

At this point, you might be throwing up a red flag and crying foul. Is it not dangerous to tell believers that their walk should be easy, and that they are always a perfect ten? With that sort of teaching how are we to encourage godly living? Won't followers of Christ live sloppy lives apart from certain restraints? You may think this sort of grace sounds too radical.

If you find yourself uncomfortable with grace, you are really struggling with the Scripture. Paul announced with great boldness, "We are more than conquerors in Christ."[11] We don't become conquerors: we *are* already conquerors by virtue of His Abiding Life in us. The Bible clearly states, "He became Sin, that we might become the righteousness of God."[12] Jesus became sin on the cross, in a moment of time, and we became fully righteous the moment we received Christ. Our righteousness is not progressive, but instantaneous. We progressively "live out" a perfect righteousness. These verses are clear and cannot be made to say anything different.

No man can force you into this moment of surrender. No book you read or message that you hear from a pulpit can push you into rest. You must simply get tired enough. You must choose to lay down the barbed wire. The writer of Hebrews states, "There remains a rest to the people of God."[13] Why continue to struggle? Why live with constant fear, always wondering if you have done enough, or if something you have done, will push God away from you?

Paul attempted to discipline himself into a life of devotion to Jesus. He threw all of his efforts into restraining self. He knew the things he should not do and yet was powerless to stop himself.[14] He knew what he should do and yet couldn't pull it off. Reeling back and forth, like a seasick sailor, he finally grabbed the side of the ship and regurgitated all his pride and self-will. Watching the disgusting mass of human waste float out to sea, he looked to the heavens and cried, "Who shall deliver me from this body of death?"[15]

The deliverance that Paul needed came through a "Who," not a "what." The Apostle thanked God through Jesus Christ for the power of His Life. What Paul could not do because of the weakness of his flesh, Jesus effortlessly performed in him.

Are you ready to take your eyes off of yourself and place them on Christ alone? Ready to become singularly focused on Jesus? When we walk according to our own abilities and strength, our focus is on many things, but when we decide that Jesus is all we need, our eyes are on Him only.

Christ's command is to abide in Him. Abiding means that we remain where God has placed us. At the very moment of conversion, we are placed in Christ. Like a fish is at home *in* the water, we are at home in Christ. We thrive and grow in the environment of Christ in us.

We can never take ourselves out of Christ, but we can lose the benefits of this high position by attempting to "live for the Lord." Like a fish *out* of water, we can flop about on the shore, choosing to center our lives on ourselves, instead of the sufficiency of Christ. The result will be pleasing to our pride but damaging to our souls.

Jesus linked intimacy with Him as the starting place of eternal activity when He said, "Apart from me you can do nothing."[16]

We can do many things. We can start projects and programs in our attempt to advance the Kingdom of God. We can restrain sin for a season by our countless strategies, but as far as He is concerned, any attempt to do these things apart from Him is all wood, hay, and stubble.

Are you prepared to shift your paradigm? Are you ready for your "Magan"? Nothing is more beautiful than a trout in a stream, when it is swimming with the current of life.

CHAPTER 9

THE MIST

Bisbee stared across the countryside. He walked beside Charlie up the dirt road toward the Old Red Barn. In the distant field lay row after row of broken corn stalks. Dotting the pasture were massive footprints left by the elephant's furious rampage. Bisbee knew that he would be back; however, he also knew he was not afraid. He was convinced he was closer to the mystery of the Well.

Bisbee was sure Marnin loved him, in spite of the Beast. In Bisbee's ugly entanglement with the Beast, Marnin's love had remained constant. Convinced of the Master's unconditional acceptance, Bisbee embraced the fact he could do nothing in his own strength to conquer the elephant. He had been outflanked and overwhelmed for the last time. For Bisbee, the years of struggling in Harness had been transformed into a burning passion to discover the mystery of the Well of Chayah.

"Good to finally give up, isn't it?"

Bisbee had forgotten that Charlie was walking next to him. A muskrat's soft paws make very little noise, especially on a dirt path. A broad smile broke out on Bisbee's face.

"No, it's great to give up! I wish I had dropped this burden years ago. I feel as light as a feather. So where are we going next?" Charlie asked.

The Traveler poked Charlie in the side. Feigning irritation, the muskrat moved away.

"You don't know?"

"No, I was under the impression that you were my guide."

"*Do you still have the map and the writings in your back pocket?*" *Charlie inquired.*

"*Since entering Charis, why?*" *Bisbee responded quickly, realizing he had forgotten all about them. He had been checking them less and less since meeting Charlie. The map, writings and his friend's letters were still in his back pocket. Why had he neglected them? Had he begun to depend on Charlie too much? He had found Charis by following the map and the writings. Did he think that he did not need them anymore? Bisbee pulled them out to reassure himself and showed them to Charlie.*

"*Just wanted to make sure you knew where they were.*"

Bisbee detected a hint of rebuke but after quieting himself decided to ignore it.

The pair continued up the grassy road until they came to an equipment shed standing next to the main barn. Climbing up on a stack of worn tractor tires, Bisbee peered into the shed through a broken window. He carefully kept his face away from the shattered glass as he waited for his eyes to adjust to the darkness. Full of rusty farm tools, the small shed was a graveyard of worn out plows and old tractor parts. The strong odor of used motor oil filled the opening. Bisbee saw a pair of large green eyes peering back at him. A flurry of feathers came rushing toward him causing Bisbee to lose his balance. Falling backwards to the ground, Bisbee landed hard on a blue salt block. Stunned, the Traveler struggled to his feet.

"*Wow! What was that?*"

"*That was Beatrice, the barn owl. Normally she's very pleasant, but doesn't like to be disturbed when she's roosting.*"

"*Well, I don't like being attacked by feathers.*"

Charlie burst into laughter.

"*What's so funny?*"

"*Bisbee, you've just faced the fury of an elephant as well as the meanness of Hugabone, don't tell me you're startled by a few feathers.*"

Unable to catch his breath, Charlie rolled off into the pasture, filling the valley with laughter.

"*Quite the sense of humor, Charlie ole boy. Go on, get it out of your system.*"

Bisbee sat down in the grass, waiting for the muskrat to exhaust himself. Leaning his back against an old rusty plow, he began chewing on a fresh piece of hay. Looking up, Bisbee saw a young collie walking past him on his way down to the stream. *The dog stopped to smell Bisbee's pant leg and raised her head long enough to be petted.*

"That's an annoying muskrat that you smell. If you'd like to chase him, he's over there in the field."

Hearing Bisbee, Charlie launched into a fresh tirade of laughter and fell back into the clover. *The dog sneezed twice and continued on his way.*

As he chewed his stalk of hay, a blue bird fluttered above, finally perching on the plow only a few feet away from Bisbee. Staring into his eyes, she began cleaning her beak on the hard metal. Feeling the cold plow against his back, Bisbee sensed the Master was doing some plowing of His own. Marnin's methods were sometimes painful, and yet Bisbee knew they were needed. Bisbee thought of all the profound things he had experienced since entering the land.

Horatio C. Goldspinner had jarred his thinking, introducing him to the value of an open mind. Passing over Crossing Bridge had given Bisbee a taste of freedom. His friendship with Charlie had taught him to be humble enough to listen to a rodent. In some strange way, even Hugabone had helped Bisbee. The fact that the Elders in Harness had sent him revealed their need to control. His exchange with the trapper had caused Bisbee to think of his family back home.

Choosing to reject his growing anxiety, Bisbee realized he was pleased with his decision to walk away from the elephant. He refused to fight him with weapons that he now knew were useless. Even the shame he had experienced from his connection with the Beast had been quickly lifted by the love and forgiveness of Marnin. It was all beginning to make perfect sense. The great discovery at the Well of Chayah was ahead of him, and Bisbee began to crave victory. Why had he waited so long to come to Charis? Charlie's earlier statement became clear: he did indeed have a lot to unlearn. After finishing her beak sharpening session, the blue bird flew away toward Broken Dam.

Refreshed from his laughing fit, Charlie started back down the trail toward the creek. Bisbee ran to catch up.

"Why are we returning to the stream?"

"You ought to know Bisbee."

Charlie stopped in full stride and turned back toward the Traveler. Placing his hands on his hips, the muskrat tightened his lips and cocked his head to the left.

"Well, are you going to look at it?"

Bisbee was puzzled. Charlie was staring at the map in the Traveler's hand.

"Just holding it, does no good. There's no magical power flowing from its pages. No comfort by simply having it close to you. I can look at a crawfish all day long, but I prefer eating it."

Bisbee saw his point. He wondered why he hesitated.

"Charlie, do I really need the map and the writings now?"

Bisbee was surprised to hear the words come out of his mouth. He apparently had become too comfortable around his new friend. Having started down this line of reasoning, Bisbee decided to continue.

"I've been thinking…"

"This doesn't sound good."

"No, listen. I have never been happier. I sense Marnin's love and closeness more than ever since crossing the Bridge. The elephant walked away in defeat just a few moments ago. I have no fear of it anymore. I'm not sure what Marnin meant about death in the land, but I feel more alive than ever. I'm not sure where the map leads or how the writings will guide me, but I'm happy right here, right now."

The muskrat frowned.

"I keep hearing the words, 'I'm not sure.' That should tell you something. Bisbee, look at me."

The Traveler looked into Charlie's eyes and the muskrat continued.

"If you think this is all there is; if you imagine the Land of Charis as just a place of grace, you are terribly mistaken. There is so much more that you do not know. The elephant walked away but not in defeat. You've taken some important steps, yet this is only the beginning of your journey. You've tasted freedom; you haven't swallowed anything. Victory over the elephant is not real to you yet. Look at me. You need to read the map and the writings!"

Bisbee struggled. A part of him knew Charlie was right; yet, he inwardly feared what Marnin had referred to as death. Maybe a taste of victory was all Bisbee cared about. If avoiding death meant laying down the map, would it be such a bad thing? Did he really need this muskrat? Maybe Horatio C Goldspinner would be better company.

Bisbee looked down to see a mist covering his feet. Mesmerized by the soft blanket surrounding his ankles, he was unaware that his grip on the map and the writings had loosened. Bisbee barely noticed the document falling to the ground and rolling into a ditch.

Suddenly the mist sent a chill up his spine. Frostbite gripped his hands as a thousand icy needles pricked his fingertips. The Traveler had never felt so cold. Panic stricken, he looked down at his empty hands. Bisbee began breathing short labored breaths as he frantically searched in the grass for the map and the writings.

Charlie's eyes saddened as he turned to walk away. Bisbee's head began to spin out of control. Nausea overcame him, forcing him to his knees. He felt like he had swallowed a handful of small jagged rocks. Without warning a cold rain driven by a north wind swept across Charis, pelting Bisbee's face. In a fit of panic, he searched the trail for Charlie, but the muskrat was gone.

Running down the path, his foot hit a root and threw him to the ground. Bisbee forced himself to vomit, jamming his finger down his throat. Crawling away from the disgusting mass did nothing to alleviate him. The driving rain continued to pelt his exposed back as the mist grew deeper. Surrounded by the thickening fog, the stench of cow manure mixed with moldy hay caused him to vomit again. Clutching his stomach, Bisbee doubled over, rolling onto his side. Crawling up next to the walnut tree, he feared he would pass out. Covered by the fog and sickened by the thought of losing the map and the writings, Bisbee began to violently shake.

Bisbee lost all sense of time, until out of the corner of his eye he saw movement on his left arm. A large black carpenter ant was crawling toward him, weaving back and forth through the hairs of his arm. In his attempt to retain consciousness, Bisbee decided to focus on the ant's busy march. Unable to cry out or move, Bisbee was trapped in a cloudy grave but the worst was yet to come.

Sensing movement in the grass, the Traveler saw something approaching. A black snake was slithering toward him. Bisbee watched in horror as it moved up the back of his leg, finally reaching his lower back. Frozen, he could do nothing to stop its advance. The snake was moving toward his head.

Bisbee closed his eyes and braced for the worst. He prayed for a quick death as he awaited the razor fangs of the serpent. Bisbee could feel the reptile's breath and the flickering of his tongue on the back of his neck. The snake coiled at his nape and whispered in his ear. The creature then slid down Bisbee's spine and vanished into the tall grass. Horrified, the Traveler's head hit the ground.

Bisbee laid motionless on the trail, in and out of consciousness throughout the night. Each time he came to, the words of the serpent cast upon his soul an impending sense of terror. The longer he thought on the statement, the less he could remember it. Finally, Bisbee's failure to recall the words frustrated him to the point of despair. How could he hear something so upsetting and yet forget it so quickly?

Conscious enough to note the shuffling of cattle, Bisbee attempted to drag himself off of the trail. If the snake didn't kill him, the massive bovine would. The last thing Bisbee remembered was wishing he was home with Avonlea.

When the Traveler finally awoke, the next morning, he was lying in a clover field just north of Crossing Bridge. Feeling the warmth of the sun on his face, Bisbee slowly opened his eyes. The strong scent of alfalfa was a welcome relief from the stench of the night before. Charlie was sitting next to him, whistling a happy song. With his eyes fixed on the lush valley, the muskrat was enjoying the beauty of Charis. Bisbee turned away, irritated by the rodent's cheerful mood.

The events of the previous night were beginning to surface in Bisbee's mind. What had the snake said? He tried again to remember but gave up. Checking his back pocket, he was surprised to find the map. Maybe he had never lost it in the first place. Perhaps it had all been just a bad dream, and that there had been no fog, no illness, and no snake.

Charlie turned toward Bisbee, abruptly ending his tune.

"What did he whisper in your ear?"

So it was not a dream. Bisbee felt as if Charlie knew what the snake had whispered in his ear. Irritated that the muskrat had left him in the mist, Bisbee decided that if he did know what the serpent had said, he would not tell Charlie. Turning toward the muskrat, Bisbee snarled.

"I can't remember."

Charlie smiled.

"Where did the attitude come from? I'm trying to help you."

Bisbee exhaled.

"Why didn't the snake bite me?" asked Bisbee.

"He did. He inflicted a wound much deeper than two puncture marks in the neck. The snake injected its venom into your mind."

"How can it affect my mind when I don't even know what it whispered?"

"The serpent did what he always does. He planted a thought. The only chance you have to rid yourself of its poison is to remember what he whispered in your ear. If you don't recall the words he said, you are doomed to fulfill them."

Bisbee felt iciness in his limbs and at the back of his neck, a clear fluid began the ooze down his spine.

"But you know what he said…"

"Oh no. It doesn't work that way. If I told you, the venom would still be in you. You have to remember for yourself."

"Does the snake have a name?"

"Oh no, you're not going to get me again. I'm already in trouble with Marnin for giving out names. Besides, knowing his name won't help you remember what he said."

"But why did the snake plant the thought in my mind?"

"Because a lie spoken out loud is understood as a deceitful thing, but a lie buried deep within the mind possesses the advantage of darkness. In the cloak of ignorance, a falsehood germinates into an attitude and then grows into a way of life."

"How did I end up here? Did you drag me off of the trail?" Bisbee asked.

Charlie looked amused.

"Really, a four-pound muskrat? No, it was the Master who rescued you."

The thought of Marnin dragging him out of the mist filled Bisbee with mixed emotions. He was grateful the Master had not left him there, but he felt shame for what he had said to Charlie about the map and the writings. Maybe he had not told Marnin about their conversation.

The muskrat looked up, "It's time you meet the People of the Wood."

"Who?"

"For heaven's sake Bisbee, clean your ears out. I said the People of the Wood. They live at the top of the hill."

"Why would I want to meet them?"

"Do you want to know what the snake whispered in your ear?"

"Yes."

"You'll remember in the Wood."

After a good long stretch, Charlie began his long walk up the hill.

Bisbee remained sitting in the grass with the map and the writings in his hands. He began to unfold them but something stopped him. Looking up the hill, he spotted Charlie nearing the Wood.

"Wait, I'm coming!" Bisbee shouted.

Soon after the fall of mighty Jericho, the Jewish nation fell into sin as a result of committing a very specific error. In the conquest of

Jericho, the army of Joshua had employed military tactics that could be described as comical. After responding to Joshua's leadership, the soldiers of Israel watched in astonishment as the walls of Jericho came tumbling down. As the soldiers shouted and the trumpets blasted, the impregnable City of Jericho crumbled like a house of cards.[1] Such futile military maneuvers had never been used against a foe of such strength. The warriors of Jehovah simply marched around the city walls for seven days, enduring the ridicule of the Canaanites.

Experiencing victory by the power of Jehovah, the troops stormed into Jericho and easily took control of the once powerful city. But then, after the excitement had died down, something sinister occurred. Tasting the thrill of conquest, they entertained a vile thought. Like a silent plague, invisible and yet as real as the rubble at their feet, a suggestion spread amongst the soldiers. Sin had crept into the camp before the dust of triumph had a chance to settle on the crumbling walls of Jericho. Pride had firmly embedded itself in the minds of the warriors. Likewise, if we believe that every enemy falls after Jericho by default, we have become susceptible to the temptation of pride.[2]

The seeds of future defeat were planted. What grievous error did the Israelites entertain? What is the hidden snare laying in the path of Charis? It is to entertain the thought, that since grace has been revealed, the Word of God is no longer needed. The great danger in the initial stages of understanding grace is believing that we possess the victory within ourselves.

Dangerous detours can be taken on the path to the Well of Chayah. Along the trail to freedom there are perilous pitfalls and crippling snares to avoid at all costs. There are devilish temptations that can overtake us if we allow ourselves to become spellbound by our release from the grip of law. At the very moment that grace is revealed, we become vulnerable to the numbing effects of pride.[3]

After their victory at Jericho, the next village they came to was tiny Ai. On the heels of triumph, the Israelites felt invincible, causing this small town to be viewed as a "push over." No prayer from Joshua's forces ascended to the heights nor was any dependence on Jehovah displayed. Dispatching a few soldiers to "take care" of this tiny town, they were crushed by the "little army" of Ai. Pride had entered... and with it death.

Early triumphs can become a trap if we begin to trust in the experience of victory, rather than in the Victor Himself. Past Victories press the "Autopilot Button," and we begin to mindlessly wander about the plane, eating peanuts and enjoying the inflight movie. Undetected, the thought enters our minds that a steady diet of Bible study is no longer needed. In a fog of paralysis, we become sick from yesterday's manna.

It is important to be thankful for the victories that God gives us; yet, we slide down a slippery slope if we neglect His Word and begin to believe in our own self-sustainability. We are only moments away from a fall, when we think we stand on solid footing. Solid footing is found in a growing understanding of God's Word.

Living in the wonder of God's grace is revealed in a moment, but abiding in the reality of His abundant supply, takes a bit longer. Do not be deceived by the momentary joy of any victory you may have experienced. The elephant of the flesh has simply run for cover. The beast will reappear, but you will discover, in time, that God has dealt with the flesh in a very specific way. It takes years for the deep abiding work of Christ to become permanently woven into the fabric of our lives.

This truth, concerning the time it takes to grow to maturity, is not meant to cloud your happy day or rain on your parade. By all means, revel in the fall of Jericho, but remember, maturity does not come instantly. At the start, the tip of the iceberg is all that is in view. Be careful not to grow cold in your faith. It is important to note that our Father is in no hurry when it comes to our growth. When God wants to grow an oak, He takes a hundred years, but when He wants a squash, He takes six months.[4] God is interested in growing us into spiritual oak trees.

The fact is we have much to learn before we possess the Promise Land. There are many enemies and dangers; yet, in the land of Canaan, the temptation to bathe in the euphoria of a past victory is strong.

To lay aside the Scripture, believing we possess a full knowledge of grace, is a grave error. A false sense of fullness causes us to push away the steak and potatoes of God's word for the moldy bread. It is like a child returning home from his first day of school, proudly announcing that there is no need for him to return for a second day. Pride springs the steel trap, and our hearts close down. As a result, we become spiritually malnourished. The "Autopilot Button" of this false notion is glowing red but to push it is to court certain disaster.

The Bible encourages us to taste and see that the Lord is good.[5] But tasting and savoring are two different things. Knowledge that floats in the head is not the same thing as victory that becomes an abiding truth within our lives. There is a huge difference between tasting reality at the start and experiencing that same reality as an ongoing experience.

There is no substitute for the essential element of growing in the knowledge of Scripture. God's Word, (our map), is to be studied diligently. The directional markings in His Word lead us to freedom from sin's power over us. There is nothing the elephant fears more than the Word of God. The Scripture's ultimate goal is to lead us into the presence of the One who gives victory. The goal of the flesh is to launch us out into the dark waters of self-reliance, in a boat with holes.

According to the Bible, the freedom that we have in Christ, has already been procured.[6] God has a process for our abiding deliverance from the power of the flesh. He works in us, according to what He has accomplished on the cross, and this mystery is not discovered quickly.

As a young boy I grew up on a farm owned by a man named Mr. Sturm. Every summer Mr. Sturm would crank up his green John Deere tractor and head out into the field to cut hay. The process of his labor was always the same. After cutting the alfalfa, he would allow it time to dry in the field. Weeks later, he would return and process the dried grass into bales. The hay bales would then have to be rolled in the field, so that they would be completely dried out before being taken to the barn. Stacking wet or damp hay in the barn would create mold and waste his crop.

Progressively discovering the truths of Scripture is the process of spiritual growth, and these "discoveries" create a sequential order. But how are we to understand these things?

Paul tells us that faith comes by hearing and hearing by the Word of God.[7] Have you ever noticed that the verse involves a two-part equation? First of all, faith comes by hearing. This "hearing" involves listening with an open heart. This is beyond just an open ear. The second half of Romans 10:17 declares plainly that it is the Word of God, which feeds faith. It is the substance of truth that nourishes faith. Our hearts are to be open to God's Word.

This process alone keeps us steadily on the path to victory. The nation of Israel crossed over the Jordan River at only one place when entering the Promise Land. They did not pick and choose where they wanted to cross. There is only one place of crossing. God's only bridge to enter the Promise Land is built on His Son and His work on The Cross, as recorded in the Bible.

Do you remember the many "paths to victory" that were presented to you before grace was revealed? Book after book was digested and yet you found no peace. A thousand trips to the altar yielded nothing more than a worn carpet and sore knees. Every promise you made to God was broken before the ink was dry on your "commitment card." You knew in your heart there had to be something more; something you were missing.

Many dangers lie on the path to the Well of Chayah, and this particular one of pride comes early in the journey. In "seeing" we become blind; in "fullness," we lose our hunger for truth. The fog appears, and we enter its crippling domain. As a result of neglecting the Word of God, spiritual withdrawal overtakes us. The serpent whispers this lie, and we shut down our hearts.

The ground required for growth is not built on the soggy bogs of decomposing past triumphs or from yesterday's Bible study. The liberating truths of the gospel are not discovered during high spiritual moments or after great victories. True victory is understanding the truths found in the Bible. Jesus stated clearly in John 8:32, "If you continue to follow Me, you will know the Truth and it is the Truth that will set you free."

By all means, rejoice in your newfound freedom but know that growth takes time. If you become disappointed in yourself, it is a reminder to stop expecting anything from yourself. Never mistake your present experience of victory as something given to you apart from Christ. Abiding victory in the life of the believer is found moment by moment by abiding in Christ. Our understanding of God's path of growth will be fully revealed in time; however, if you think you're there, you're not. If you believe you know, you don't. If you imagine you've arrived, you are adrift in the fog.

So grab the oars and begin rowing toward the Lighthouse. You will never discover the joy of walking on the solid ground of God's word, while floating on the uncertain waters of experiences. The food you need is found on the shore. One last warning: if you allow the currents to take you away from the shore, there is no telling what sandy beach you may land on. The mist is a dangerous place to be, and its destination is even worse.

CHAPTER 10

GLASSY POND

Carefully placing the map and writings in his back pocket, Bisbee started up the hill after Charlie. The Traveler kept one eye out for woodchuck holes as the prospect of reinjuring his ankle played on his mind. Bisbee paused to catch his breath, only to have the landscape take it away from him.

Soft green pastures climbed to a small wooded area on top of the hill overlooking the Land of Charis. Towering pines waved in the breeze. Bisbee had never seen such a beautiful shade of green. He recalled seeing the wooded area when he had climbed over the fence from the cemetery only a few days earlier. He had noticed a neatly cut trail leading into the forest. It was densely wooded, and it had occurred to Bisbee that it would be a great place to explore.

Who lived in The Wood? Having just crossed over Living Stream, it was obvious that these people did not actually live in Charis. What significance could they play in a Land that they only viewed from a distance? Whatever it was, the Traveler knew there were things to be learned in The Wood.

Bisbee was a "cards on the table" sort of man, so he naturally wondered why the muskrat had a habit of being so secretive. A simple explanation from Charlie might eliminate the need for a trip into The Wood. Bisbee was frustrated that his friend knew what the snake had whispered in his ear and would not share it with him. Why not just tell him and be done with it? Apparently, the worrisome rodent enjoyed a good game of "cat and mouse," or perhaps it was just that Charlie enjoyed watching him struggle.

Bisbee smelled smoke and looked up. A dark plume was billowing high into the sky. As it crested the treetops, the smoke appeared to be the color of red cedar but changed to a pale yellow the higher it climbed. Was this the source of the fog he had experienced the night before? He thought of asking Charlie, but Bisbee knew he had to connect the dots without any help from his Guide. The mental discipline of thinking had never been encouraged in Harness, so he was a little rusty at the art of contemplative deduction.

"Now where did Charlie go?" Bisbee muttered to himself.

Finally spotting him in the tall grass, he paused to study the agile muskrat. The morning sun was dancing off Charlie's soft, black fur, as he bounded effortlessly through the clover. Occasionally, the muskrat would stop and smell the air and then playfully roll down the hill at break-neck speed. Against all efforts to the contrary, Bisbee was growing even more fond of him.

He realized Charlie was right: he had been foolish to think Charis was simply about release from his own misery. Bisbee was beginning to see how selfish he had been his whole life. What was his motivation for coming to this Land? Was his primary goal nothing more than a self-centered fixation and his own desire to be free? Bisbee was convinced that the Land of Charis possessed a design grander than just his personal freedom or deliverance from Harness.

"Are you gonna let me catch up?" Bisbee called out.

Charlie turned back toward him, placing his paw over his mouth.

"Quiet, we don't want them to know we're coming."

Bisbee smiled and raised his voice.

"Then maybe we shouldn't be walking in broad daylight through an open field."

Charlie shook his head in dismay. Bisbee regretted that he had chosen to throw a barb at his Guide. The muskrat continued up the hill.

As they approached the forest, Bisbee noticed a grove of birch trees lining the border of The Wood. Giant quaking aspens towered over the birches, sheltering them from the soft morning sun. A gentle, east wind blew, causing the aspens to break into a nervous dance. A small family of deer appeared at the edge of the forest. Lifting their noses, they turned and leapt into the blackness of the dense overgrowth.

Charlie stopped suddenly.

"This is where I leave you. I'll see you back in Charis. Don't stay in The Wood for more than a few hours. Nothing is to be trusted."

The muskrat turned and retreated down the hill.

Bisbee cupped his hands to his mouth and called after him.

"*Why only a few hours?*"

Charlie stopped and turned back toward Bisbee.

"*Because if you stay too long, you'll never come out. And Bisbee, one more thing, beware of Glassy Pond.*"

Bisbee looked back toward the forest. Turning to ask Charlie for an explanation, all he saw was an empty field. He searched left and then right, but the muskrat had vanished.

He longed to run back down the hill and reenter Charis. Looking into the Valley, he saw Marnin sitting on the dam. His feet were dangling loosely off the wall as a breeze lifted his long white hair into the air. Peaceful and at ease, the Master's eyes were fixed on The Traveler. How could Marnin be at such peace when Bisbee felt he was so vulnerable?

Bisbee wanted to run to him. Nothing would have felt better at that moment than an embrace. For reasons unknown to Bisbee, the Master always seemed far away when he needed him most. With the dark forest behind him, Marnin made no move to join Bisbee in the adventure. Did he not care what might happen to him in The Wood or was this a test of some sort? Whatever the reason, Marnin remained on the dam, swinging his legs back and forth.

It was always hard for Bisbee to take his eyes off the Master, but in the present situation, what choice did he have? This trip into the forest must be a part of his journey to the Well. Turning back toward The Wood, he forced himself to enter the darkness.

Bisbee reminded himself to be as quiet as possible, but the sound of dead branches and dry acorns cracking under his feet made any hope of silence an illusion. Walking past the aspens, Bisbee discovered a small, well-worn trail. Lining the path were rotten tree stumps filled with busy carpenter ants. With every step down the trail, the forest grew darker and darker as the rays of the sun battled through the foliage to reach the forest floor. Growing weary, Bisbee spotted a stump that looked like a good place to rest, only to discover that it was too rotten to support his weight. He had lifted his foot to kick it over when he heard a voice above him.

"*I wouldn't do that if I were you.*"

Bisbee never saw who spoke. His foot sunk into the porous wood, sending a huge swarm of angry wasps into the air. Confident of their target, the wasps attacked, filling Bisbee's shirt and pants.

The first instinct of the terrified Traveler was to run, but his foot caught a small tree root, and he tumbled onto the mossy forest floor. Lying there on a soft mattress of green, he braced for the inevitable experience of being stabbed with hundreds of tiny razor sharp needles. The wasps lifted their stingers and buried them deep into Bisbee's flesh. His breath quickened, as his heart throbbed within his chest. Was this the moment of death of which the Master had spoken?

Glassy eyed, Bisbee stared into the treetops, but the pain he had anticipated never arrived. Much to Bisbee's surprise and relief, there was a warm sensation of pleasure, which accompanied each sting. Falling deep into a trance, he lay motionless on the forest floor. Bisbee was quite content to experience each passing moment of intense pleasure.

Suddenly, he felt pressure on his stomach. The wasps immediately retracted their stingers and began flying away.

Bisbee looked down toward his torso and saw a strange creature sitting on his chest. Its black, marble-shaped eyes watched the rise and fall of Bisbee's chest. The creature's small mouse-like ears listened intently to the Traveler's breath as its round, white face twitched from side to side. Bisbee blinked. The creature blinked. Bisbee leaned forward to get a better look. The creature also leaned forward until they were almost touching noses. Whatever was on Bisbee's stomach could stand it no longer.

"Boo!"

Bisbee screamed, sending the creature rolling off into the leaves, laughing hysterically. In a flash, it was back, serious as death, and standing again on Bisbee's chest. The Traveler had never seen anyone transition out of laughter and back into "serious," that quickly. After sitting down on Bisbee's chest, the little animal spoke in a deep Scottish brogue.

"So you must be Bisbee. Charlie said you were coming."

"And who are you?" Bisbee inquired.

"Forgive me, where are my manners?"

Perching on his hind legs, he bowed his head in a stately manner.

"I am an opossum. The name is Pete."

Pete the opossum

"*Oh, you're a possum.*"

"*No, I believe I was quite clear. I am an opossum. Are you from the back country?*"

"*Yes, well, not originally.*"

"*Why is it so difficult for you to pronounce the "O" in opossum?*"

Bisbee thought it strange that Pete was so particular about such things, but he decided everyone deserves the respect of being properly identified. Dealing with a temperamental marsupial was the least of Bisbee's present struggles.

Pete smiled, revealing a row of sharp, cat-like teeth, trailing down a long narrow snout. The fur on his back was brown and appeared to be quite soft.

"*Go ahead and touch it. It is very soft.*"

Great, Bisbee thought, another animal that can read my thoughts.

"*I'm good. The teeth do concern me a little.*"

After opening his mouth, a full finger's length, Pete reached down and gently tapped Bisbee's arm with his teeth.

"*See? You've got nothing to worry about. I have complete control of them.*"

The opossum hopped off of Bisbee's chest and began digging for acorns. Bisbee recalled Charlie's warning and decided to be cautious with his new acquaintance.

"*The wasps weren't what you expected, were they?*" *Pete had anticipated Bisbee's next question.*

"*No. In fact I was a little disappointed that you interrupted their attack.*"

"I saved your life. A few more minutes and you would have been permanently paralyzed."

Pete saw that his new friend needed further explanation.

"You, sir, are in The Wood. You need to understand that everything in this forest is about you."

"And what's wrong with that?"

"Pleasure over a long period of time, Bisbee, will lead to paralysis, which in the case of the wasps is exactly four minutes and thirty-two seconds."

Bisbee was impressed. Pete continued.

"You must be careful. Danger lurks behind every tree and in every bush. This forest is filled with temptations."

Pete lifted his nose and smelled the air.

"We're making too much noise. The People of Glassy Pond will hear us," Bisbee said.

Pete smiled again.

"Did Charlie tell you that?"

"Yes."

"He doesn't know the People of Glassy Pond like I do. They're mostly deaf."

"Really?"

"Actually, when they arrive their hearing is quite normal, but the longer they live at Glassy Pond, the deafer they become. The process is so gradual, that most are unaware that it is even happening.

"We need to be going. We only have a few hours of sunlight and you've got a lot to see."

Bisbee hesitated, remembering Charlie's warning. Could he trust this little ball of fur and teeth? At this point, he had no one else. Bisbee struggled to his feet, brushing the leaves off of his chest.

"Pete, wait up, I'm coming."

As the tree cover thickened, so did the dampness of the forest. Occasionally a deer ran across the trail. A strong scent of white pine hung in the air, reminding Bisbee of the forests back in Harness. Large plump blackberries hung off the branches of the bushes that lined the trail. Bisbee resisted picking them. If the sting of a wasp could paralyze, he shuttered to think what a single berry could do to him. He desired their pleasure but feared the paralysis that might follow.

The Wood fascinated and terrified Bisbee all at the same time. Something mysterious lay in the branches and crept across the forest floor. Bisbee was *disturbed and yet captivated by its powerful attraction. Soft, cushiony ledges grew out of every tree trunk. Deep green in color, they begged Bisbee to sit down and rest. Pete turned back toward The Traveler.*

"Don't even think about it, Bisbee. Once you sit down, you'll never get up."

The trees began swaying back and forth as a feeling of intoxication overcame Bisbee. The Traveler's ears began to itch. He felt himself beginning to lose control. Pete stooped down to smell a footprint.

"We're getting close. Do you know how to play dead?"

"No."

"I do."

The opossum let out a gurgling sound and curled up next to a birch tree. Pete lay motionless in the leaves, releasing a putrefying odor, which caused Bisbee to turn away in disgust. After several minutes of dead stillness, the opossum hopped to his feet.

"Pretty good stuff, huh?"

"Is playing dead a requirement?" asked Bisbee.

"No. I just wanted you to know I could do it." A broad smile broke out on the opossum's face.

Bisbee shook his head. A sense of humor at a time like this seemed out of place but maybe a good laugh was just what he needed. Something to shake him out of this feeling of…well, he could not identify what he was feeling.

Since entering The Wood, he had experienced the warmth of a low-grade fever. Oddly, he enjoyed it. His senses seemed heightened. It was as if he were a fly entangled in a spider's web with no desire to free himself. On the contrary, he felt like grabbing the sticky strands and wrapping himself tighter within its hold.

He had forgotten all about his friends and family. Even Charlie was fading quickly from his mind. Marnin seemed like a distant memory. In fact, Bisbee found that all he was thinking about was… himself.

Pete looked up at the Traveler and immediately saw the dilemma. He knew from past experience that there was nothing he could do to cure Bisbee's state of comatose. They just had to keep moving.

"We should climb a tree. I hear them coming."

Pete spotted a stately sugar maple and began to clumsily climb its branches. Bisbee stood at base of the tree as the possum repeatedly fell at his feet. Each time Pete shook himself off, smiled, and began climbing again. Tired of the possum's pathetic attempt to climb the maple, he finally threw the possum over his shoulder

*and began climbing. Pete clamped his teeth into Bisbee's neck, which caused The
Traveler to regain a higher level of consciousness.*

*"Maybe you should work on your climbing skills instead of wasting your
time playing dead." The possum just grunted.*

*Finally reaching what appeared to be a solid limb, the pair sat down. Covered
by foliage but still able to clearly see their surroundings, Pete and Bisbee settled
into a silent anticipation.*

*A natural theater in the shape of a horseshoe lay beneath them. The raised
platform in the middle of the arena gave Bisbee a sense that this theater was
indeed for the purpose of entertainment. The arena sat empty, except for an
occasional deer passing through. The deer seemed to be anxiously awaiting an
event of some kind.*

"Do you hear it?"

*Pete craned his ear toward the east as he scanned the underbrush. Bisbee
heard nothing. He was about to compliment Pete on his keen sense of hearing,
when he heard it too. Actually, he felt it before he heard it. The leaves around
them broke into a hypnotic dance as the sound grew louder and louder. Low tones
of a steady drumbeat vibrated the forest floor.*

*Then, as if appearing out of nowhere, he saw them. Row after row of Little
People marched into the open-air theater. They were all the same height as they
marched in perfect alignment. The Little People reminded Bisbee of a well-oiled
machine. Rocking back and forth to the beat of the drum, they filled the arena.
Pete handed Bisbee an old spyglass that had been wedged in a branch of the maple.*

*The Traveler had never seen anything like them. Their heads were abnormally
large in proportion to their bodies and their hair was parted down the middle,
waxed back with a shiny substance. The most fascinating thing about the Little
People was their ears. Beet red in color, they were swollen and cracked. Irritated
to the point of constant itching, the Little People dug their fingernails deep into
their earlobes.*

Dropping the eyeglass to his side, Bisbee turned to Pete.

"Look at those ears."

*A red-breasted robin joined them on the limb and after smiling at Bisbee,
nestled into a perched position to enjoy the show. She seemed to admire their
red ears.*

*Suddenly, the beat of the drum broke into full orchestra. Bisbee had never
heard such beautiful melodies. Perfect in pitch and flawless in delivery, the show*

had begun. The Traveler sat motionless, watching the scene unfold. The crowd swayed in perfect unison to the rhythmic tempo. As the music subsided, a man sitting in the crowd rose to his feet and walked to the stage.

Shouts of excitement reverberated through the tree limbs, but Bisbee noticed their mouths were closed. Scanning the crowd to discover the source of the thunderous verbiage, Bisbee was shocked to realize that the sound was coming from their ears. They appeared to be shouting with their ears to the little man who had walked onto the stage.

What happened next can only be described as a celebratory dance between crowd and speaker. The little man on the stage spoke soft words that were amplified in their ears. In return, the crowd smiled back, nodding vigorously. Keeping them in rapt attention, the one on the stage calmly continued speaking. Pete turned toward his new friend.

"Watch their ears."

Bisbee lifted the spyglass and focused his attention on their red, irritated ears. The scratching had stopped, and the redness was slowly dissipating. A deep sense of relief passed through the assembly like a wave, causing the crowd to fall into a hypnotic trance. The healing effect seemed to be somehow caused by whatever the speaker was saying. The ears of the Little People appeared to be completely healed.

At that point, whatever the Little Man proclaimed, was quietly acknowledged with nods and smiles. Bisbee found himself beginning to nod along with them, when, without notice, it all ended. Vanishing into the forest underbrush, the people of Glassy Pond disappeared.

"You don't understand anything you just saw, do you?"

Bisbee did not hear a word Pete had spoken. Staring into the Wood, a hollow, empty feeling came over Bisbee. How could a gathering, so impressive, leave him so flat and yet craving for more?

"I'd better get you out of here."

Satisfied with her daily dose of entertainment, the robin flew away. She would return the next day.

Bisbee stared into the theater, trying to grasp what he had just seen. Who were these Little People and why were their ears so red and irritated? The speaker's words seemed so shallow, and yet the crowd received such relief from them. The powerful performance had motivated a skeletal emptiness. Impressive in the moment, empty in the aftermath.

Bisbee heard a cracking sound. The limb he and Pete had been sitting on snapped, and he found himself crashing through the branches of the old maple. One by one, the branches broke as he descended. Bisbee landed on a large rock and then rolled off into the leaves. Moments later Pete hit the same rock and was knocked unconscious. Bisbee rose up on all fours and was amazed that no pain had accompanied the fall. Unexpectedly, the landing was soft. Looking over at Pete, he assumed he was again playing dead.

"Good day, sir."

The Little People

Bisbee looked up and standing before him was one of the people of Glassy Pond. He was dressed in a soft green shirt with gold buttons and brown corduroy pants, falling just above his ankles. He was wearing shoes, without the need of socks since the hair from his ankles filled his shoes. He was ordinary in appearance except for two particular features. His head blocked out the sun, and his ears reminded Bisbee of strawberries drying on the bush. After a mutual inspection, the Little Man spoke.

"Quite a fall you took there."

"Yes, but I think I'm still in one piece."

Standing up, Bisbee brushed the dry leaves off of his shirt.

"It appears your little friend didn't fare so well."

Pete was still lying on the rock. A small trickle of blood was flowing from the back of the opossum's head. Bisbee knew he should check on his friend but the Little Man, who stood before him, commanded his attention.

"He'll be fine. Come walk with me."

"But I should check on him..."

The Little Man had already started down the trail. Bisbee looked down at Pete lying motionless on the rock. He should have picked a better branch, thought Bisbee. He noticed the blood was still flowing from Pete's wound and had traveled down his coat. What did the opossum mean to him anyway? Ignoring the wound, Bisbee turned and caught up with the stranger.

"I have something for you."

The Little Man handed Bisbee a book, hard bound with silver pages. It was an impressive gift with a colorful cover and illustrated chapters. Bisbee lifted the book to his nose and breathed in deeply. He loved the smell of new books. He turned to thank him and found that the Little Man was headed down Broader Trail. Turning back toward Bisbee, he smiled.

"Follow me and I'll show you a wonderful place to read. It's quiet and peaceful. We call it Glassy Pond."

At the mention of Glassy Pond, Bisbee stepped back. Red warning flags dropped out of the sky, landing in the deep recesses of the Traveler's mind but for the life of Bisbee, he could not remember what the warning was about. What danger could there be at a place so pleasantly named? The sweet numbing effect of The Wood had done its work and pushed back Charlie's admonition. With eyes glazed over and with the apparent absence of clear thinking, Bisbee followed the Little Man down the trail.

They walked until they came to an opening in the thicket leading down to a large pond. The Traveler had never seen a body of water like Glassy Pond. Perfectly reflective, there was not a ripple on it, not a single bubble rising to its surface. Was there nothing living in its depths? How deep did the waters go? Turning to thank the Little Man, Bisbee discovered that he had disappeared into The Wood. Bisbee found a soft, green spot underneath a willow and sat down. Pulling his shoes off, he placed his tired feet in the Pond.

Bisbee was mesmerized as he read chapter after chapter of the book that the Little Man had given him. All the things he had ever desired were promised to him in the pages before him. Reading the book made Bisbee feel good about himself, and what could be wrong with that? Eye weary, he placed the book in the grass and when he did, a strange thing occurred. His ears began to itch. After a few minutes he picked the book back up and discovered the irritation had gone away.

As he poured over its pages, he thought of the map and the writings, which were still in his back pocket. A twinge of guilt came over Bisbee. He found himself enjoying this book more than he ever had Marnin's writings. Pushing aside these negative thoughts, he continued reading. The book seemed to know the things that Bisbee needed to hear. He read for what seemed like hours.

The red-breasted robin that had joined Bisbee in the maple, landed in a branch near the Traveler's reading spot. The little bird began chirping wildly as she witnessed Bisbee slumping over in the grass. The Traveler had dropped the book and was staring into Glassy Pond. Gazing at his own reflection, he became unresponsive to the bird flying about his head. The robin quickly flew off to find Pete.

Bisbee was in a dangerous situation. Unable to move or speak, all he could do was stare adoringly at his own reflection in the water. Unaware of his surroundings, the image in the water became more beautiful to him with every passing moment. The Traveler was trapped at Glassy Pond.

"Come on Bisbee, snap out of it."

Pete had arrived and was shaking Bisbee's arm but with no success. Jumping on Bisbee's back, the opossum tapped his neck gently with his teeth. His skin was cold and clammy and Pete knew that Bisbee was close to being trapped at Glassy Pond. The opossum turned toward the robin.

"Go tell Marnin."

She flew off to find the Master.

Within moments, large raindrops began to fall and as each drop landed, it disturbed the placid water of Glassy Pond. Bisbee's reflection began to blur. Pete stepped back and watched in wonder. How loving Marnin was to send the rain and recover His follower from the shallow waters of Glassy Pond.

Bisbee slowly turned toward Pete. Fearful he would look back into the waters, Bisbee closed his eyes and held out his hand.

"Get me out of here, quick."

Walking up the bank, Bisbee glanced to his left and saw hundreds of the shiny books scattered along the shoreline. He wondered why he missed them coming in. Is this how Travelers become People of Glassy Pond?

"Wait Pete, what about the others who have been trapped here? Can't we rescue them?"

"No. They have to decide to leave on their own, and the longer they are here, the harder it is to leave."

Bisbee had had enough of this place. Never again would he waste his time at Glassy Pond reading a book that only spoke of things that he wanted to hear.

Pete led Bisbee back to the trail leading out of The Wood. They passed by the wasp nest still lying on the ground. The spell cast by the Wood was loosening its grip with every step down the path. Bisbee hung his head.

"Pete, I'm sorry."

Pete turned around and hugged Bisbee's leg. Looking down to avoid Pete's eyes, he saw the blood on his coat and felt ashamed. The opossum had proved to be a true friend.

"Thank you for rescuing me."

"You're more than welcome, but you need to thank the robin. The rain came because she alerted Marnin."

Bisbee looked into the treetops, but the little bird was nowhere to be seen.

"How's your head?"

Pete smiled.

"I'm fine. You know I was playing dead."

Bisbee did not know whether to believe him, he was just happy his friend had recovered.

"Pete, I'm ready to listen. Tell me about this place. Who are these people? I never want to come back here again."

"The People of Glassy Pond think they are inhabitants of Charis, but they are not. They believe they follow Marnin, but they themselves are the focus of their own adoration. They believe Marnin exists for them and their benefit. Pleasure and prosperity are their mantras. Glassy Pond is their indoctrination site. The book you received contains portions of Marnin's writings, but the Master's writings are twisted to agree with their way of thinking. Glassy Pond is an inch deep and mile wide, yet people drown in it everyday."

Pete paused long enough to make sure Bisbee was listening and then he continued.

"*The People of Glassy Pond claim promises that Marnin never made. Their ears burn to hear these so-called "promises." Satisfied with the illusion of falsehoods, they are convinced nothing but good can come to them. Should I go on?*"

"*No, I understand.*" *Bisbee was sickened at the thought that he had been tempted to stay in the Wood.*

"*How does Marnin view them?*" *asked Bisbee.*

"*He loves them, but His heart breaks because He knows they're still in bondage to themselves.*"

"*Sad.*"

"*It's more than sad, it's tragic. To believe you follow Marnin and yet allow yourself to be deceived into worshiping an image of yourself, is a pathetically tragic situation. They are held in the bondage of self-absorption.*"

"*But I saw a sign in the arena about being free.*"

"*They believe they are free, but their freedom consists of following their own desires and dreams.*" *Pete responded.* "*They imagine Marnin came to fulfill their lives. Freedom in their minds means immediate deliverance from any present distress. The true freedom of Charis is something quite different.*"

"*I can't wait to get out of here.*"

As they approached the edge of The Wood, Bisbee saw Charlie waiting in the field. Pete stopped and looked up at the Traveler.

"*Don't ever come back here, Bisbee. The snake lied to you in the fog.*" *And then, after nodding to Charlie, the opossum turned and disappeared into the forest. In that moment, Bisbee remembered what the serpent had whispered in his ear.*

"*You don't need the map and the writings.*"

Bisbee quickly reached into his pocket, and pulled them out. Opening them slowly, new eyes gazed at the contents. He would never neglect them again.

Bisbee and Charlie walked down the hill in silence. Suddenly, the thunderous bellowing of an elephant erupted from deep within The Wood. Startled, Bisbee almost fell to the ground. Turning back toward the forest, the Monster had emerged from The Wood and was standing in the birch grove. Bisbee leaned forward, making sure he was seeing correctly. The elephant had turned green.

A full understanding of grace will transform our values and reorganize our priorities. By focusing on the life of Jesus in us, the orientation of our lives will progressively shift away from self and onto the person of Jesus Christ. This radical reversal from "self-serving concerns" to "God-glorifying ends" is the result of spiritual growth. The longer we walk with Christ, the greater our thirst will be for Him. Concern for our own desires will die a beautiful death.

However, before this reversal takes place, there is a danger to avoid; a false teaching that is as appealing as a flower is to a bee. What is this danger that encamps itself in the wooded mountaintops surrounding the Land of Grace? This is a falsehood, with growing popularity that determines God's purpose as one to serve us at our every beck and call.

This perilous path of instruction postulates the "clever" notion that if the correct lever is pulled, heaven will release a watershed of "blessings" on the much deserving saint. Those who promote such ideology, tell their followers that all that is needed is enough faith or a well-oiled prayer life in order to "activate" God's "destiny" for their lives. Grace is proclaimed as a means to acquire the blessings of health, wealth and a life free from potholes.

"Name it and claim it, brother!"

These false teachers are easy to identify. Dazzling crowds with new teachings, never before "revealed," these modern day "prophets of prosperity" draw attention to their self-assigned authority rather than declare biblical truth. After claiming that they possess the "anointing," whatever they speak is instantly raised to the level of Scripture. A "word from the Lord" is "prophesied" by the "anointed one," without the Bible ever being opened, and if it is, the passage of Scripture presented is twisted out of measure to the degree that it does not even resemble its original message.

Following Christ has nothing to do with filling our bank accounts, granting our dreams or healing every aching joint. The life that God offers us is not centered in our pursuit of pleasures or prosperity. Christianity is about Christ. If it were about our desires, God owes an apology to the Old Testament saints, New Testament apostles, and the majority of early Christians. The "thorn" in Paul's flesh would have been instantly pulled out, if Christianity were about his comfort. If the goal of the Gospel was to cater to our every whim, then the martyrs of the church, in all ages, were obviously wrong to lay down their lives.[1]

Paul warned Timothy that in the last days, men would desire teachers that would tell them what they wanted to hear. He described them as "lovers of their own selves."[2] These false teachers would, in Paul's words, "scratch" the "itchy ears" of those who would follow them.[3]

It is important at this point to stop and ask some tough questions. Are we chasing after God with ulterior motives? In other words, is our pursuit of Jesus nothing more than a well-designed attempt to advance our own selfish ends?[4] Have we become master negotiators in the spiritual realm, promising God the world for a bag of peanuts?

The elephant of carnality is right at home in this self-serving, self-glorifying environment. Changing to the color of green, he sits comfortably in this sub-culture of excess. The peanuts of self-promotion are extra salty, just the way the elephant likes them. How did we get so far away from the true Gospel of Christ? The answer is quite simple.

When Adam and Eve sinned, their first impulse was not to murder, become angry, or even complain about each other. Their immediate response was an awareness of their nakedness.[5] Curious isn't it? The first couple was naked before the fall. Did Adam not know Eve was naked? Of course he did. Was Eve unaware that Adam had not "dressed" for the day? She was fine with his choice of attire, or should I say, lack thereof.

They both enjoyed the physical beauty of the other's body. Did the entrance of sin interrupt this mutual enjoyment? I do not think so. Something deeper had happened and it had nothing to do with what the other party looked like. A closer examination of the crime scene is needed.

As a result of disobeying God, the first couple ran for cover. When Adam leapt behind a nearby bush, his concern was not to cover Eve with a fig leaf: it was to cover his own nakedness. Likewise, Eve did not run to cover Adam. Her concern was to cover her own nakedness.[6]

Instead of keeping each other at the forefront of their thinking, each shifted their focus completely on themselves. In a moment of radical transformation, the psyche of Adam and Eve changed. Never again would either command the full attention of the other.

Adam was not overly concerned in making sure Eve picked out a fashionable leaf and Eve did not scurry off to the mall to fill Adam's closet. The focus of their attention had undergone a major paradigm shift. Adam thought only of Adam and Eve thought only of Eve. Eyes, that once looked outward, enjoying God's glory and creation, now turned inward as the first couple both became conscious of self. Self-consciousness was their new reality, with a default mode of self-centeredness.

What was God's response after sin had entered the human race? It was to search out His first man and in doing so He asked the question, "Adam, where are you?"[7] The question was for the benefit of Adam, since God obviously knew where he was. Adam hid in shame from his loving Creator.

The First Man had been created for the purpose of intimacy with his Creator, but henceforth he would attempt to find fulfillment by the pursuit of fleshly endeavors.

It does not require a leap of imagination to realize that we are living in the midst of Paul's warning concerning the last days.[8] Fast-forward to our present religious culture, and it is easy to identify this same preoccupation with self. If we fall into the trap of believing that we are the center of all things, then it is only natural to conclude that God's plan is to prosper us in the manner we see fit.

We all have a natural desire to live a "happy life," which causes this sort of teaching to become a deceitful trap. The thought that God would allow us to suffer is offensive to a "selfie" culture. Human reasoning is often used to justify this shallow approach with the following statement: "We want the blessings of health and wealth for our own offspring: certainly our Heavenly Father is no less benevolent." But this statement is nothing more than an attempt to understand God according to our earthly vantage point. We have no authority to "speak" anything into reality. We possess no right to "claim" prosperity over our lives.

The Apostles were hated, hunted, and eventually all martyred, except John.[9] The teaching that God would never allow His children to suffer is a travesty to the men and women who have sacrificed their lives for the Gospel of Jesus Christ over the centuries.

The writer of Hebrews, in the eleventh chapter, presents to us the stories of men and women who possessed great faith. Conquests are described in the early part of the chapter, but it is important to note that the victories they experienced were not about selfish gain. The mouths of lions were shut, the armies of the enemies were routed, and mothers received their dead back to life. The triumphs these men and women experienced, involved following God's directives, not their self-centered desires.

In stark contrast, the second half of the chapter tells the stories of cruel mockings, beatings and imprisonments. These men and women who trusted God were destitute, afflicted and tormented. Rather than living in plush residences, they resided in caves, deserts and dens. Hiding out in mountains, the Bible declares that the world was not worthy of their shining lights.[10]

God is the center of all things. When grace is properly understood and received, He will be the center of our lives, which means that He decides how our lives ultimately play out. Whatever brings Him glory is the heartthrob of the soul set free.

To stare into Glassy Pond and be snared in the trap of focusing on self is a most devilish scheme. The beast is right at home among the timbers of this approach to God. The Enemy has whispered a hideous lie in the Wood, and there are many who never escape its clutches. There are numerous shallow wells in Christianity, and this one is as deep as a puddle and just as muddy.

CHAPTER 11

SHALLOW WELLS

The late afternoon sun was descending as Charlie and Bisbee made their way down from The Wood. Bisbee's ankle had once again begun to swell, and he grimaced with each step down the hill. The Traveler scanned the valley for Marnin, but he was nowhere to be found. Bisbee's head was spinning with questions, and he knew Marnin would know the answers. The question was... would he give them?

It seemed that every step took him further away from getting the answers that he sought. He began to sense that something or someone was opposing him. After all he had been through, was he strong enough to walk the final mile? The rider on the elephant flashed across his mind. Bisbee was tired and frustrated.

As they approached the bottom of the hill, Charlie ran ahead and dove into the stream. After running his fingers through his hair, Bisbee picked up a stone and tossed it in Charlie's direction. He was not in the mood for a disappearing Guide.

"Hey, where are you going?"

He finally spotted Charlie downstream, sunning himself on the west bank. Bisbee put his hand to his mouth, intending to yell at the lazy muskrat when he noticed a woman sitting on the east bank of Living Stream. She was staring into the passing water. Her face was partially covered by her long brown hair, which almost touched the ground. She wore a soft white cotton dress, bordered with light blue fringes and large puffy sleeves. A single gold medallion hung from her delicate neck. She seemed almost angelic.

Bisbee walked toward the young lady and gently cleared his throat so as not to startle her. Stopping at what he felt was a safe distance from her, Bisbee sat down.

The mysterious woman held a single white daisy in her left hand. One by one she plucked the soft petals and then dropped them in the water. Watching each petal float downstream, she seemed tormented by their departure.

After tossing the last petal of the flower into the water, the woman lifted her head. She brushed back her hair, and Bisbee could see a tear flowing down her cheek. His heart almost stopped. It was Avonlea.

Bisbee wanted to speak, but his voice was lost in the emotion of what he was experiencing. An east wind blew, throwing strands of Avonlea's hair into the air. He could hold back no longer.

"Avonlea, is it really you?"

"Oh Bisbee, I've missed you."

Tears filled her eyes as Bisbee struggled to find his breath. Was she real or an illusion? Had he spent too much time in The Wood? Bisbee thought back to the berries he had been tempted to eat and was thankful he had resisted the forbidden fruit. Wiping the tears from his eyes, he looked back at his wife.

"Avonlea… What are you doing here? Did they try to hurt you?"

"Bisbee, we haven't much time, take my hand."

He reached out, eager to feel the touch of her soft skin. Gazing into her eyes, Bisbee became light-headed. Like lightening bolts flashing across a dark summer sky, images of Harness began to unfold in Bisbee's mind…

"Bisbee, wake up, it's almost Meeting Time."

Mitch stood outside his friend's bedroom window singing his announcement over and over again. Bisbee was glad he had been awakened, even though Mitch's singing was getting under his skin. In less than an hour, the Old Barn would overflow with the inhabitants of Harness, and the Elders would expect him to be there. Bisbee thought about waking Avonlea, but he knew she would not come. She had long ago lost interest in the weekly gathering.

Walking down the path to the Old Barn, Bisbee thought about the many times that he and Mitch had shared this moment. They had been friends since childhood.

"Do you think today will be any different?" asked Mitch.

"No." Bisbee knew exactly where his friend was going with this conversation. Mitch continued.

"Then why do we go?"

"Because it's expected. Don't we have this conversation every time we walk down this path?"

"Yes, and I'll quit asking when you give me a good answer." Sharing a smile, they continued down the trail.

Bisbee had a theory about the meetings, but he was not ready to share it with his friend. He knew The Elders well enough not to question their methods or authority. He feared Macafee knew of his suspicions, and the last thing he wanted was to draw his friend into the controversy. He would talk to Mitch when he had firm footing for his allegations.

Arriving at the Meeting Place, they entered through a large door. The pungent smell of moldy hay always reminded Bisbee of death. Finding a quiet corner, he climbed up onto a stack of hay bales. Mitch wandered into the crowd, greeting his many friends. Bisbee was proud of his friend, and he secretly wished he could be more like him. Everybody liked Mitch.

Bisbee watched with curiosity, as Tourgen, one of the Elders, crossed the floor and engaged Mitch in conversation. This had not been the first time Bisbee had witnessed an encounter between the two, and their growing friendship troubled him. When asked about it, Mitch simply changed the subject. Bisbee concluded that the topic of their talk was none of his business; after all, he had his own secrets. Mitch turned to locate his friend, causing Bisbee to slide deeper into the corner.

The Old Barn was spacious. Hay was stored along the sides as well as in the loft overhead. Thick wooden beams ran throughout, and tiny holes in the old metal roof allowed specks of light to shine in, creating a star-like scene. The beams on the second story were prime seating to view the activities of the Gathering Times. Occasionally, mice could be seen playing in the loft, but no one seemed to care. Located at the front of the Old Barn, high above the meeting floor, was a single window, which allowed sunlight to fill an otherwise dark chamber.

He thought about the years he had spent there, and he wondered if it had all been a colossal waste of time and energy. Each week the same reoccurring movement of dead activity would play itself out.

The people of Harness would enter the Meeting Place. A man-made cloud of dust, caused by the shuffling of feet, would then dance in the sunbeams. After the meeting was over and the people had filed out, the dust would then settle back onto the barn floor. To Bisbee, all the efforts in the Old Barn seemed as *asphyxiating as that cloud of dust. Their endless activities were like minute particles of nothingness, falling into the crevices of a yesterday, that no one would remember. Bisbee sneezed.*

The order of the meetings never varied. A large jar, hand molded from clay that had been taken from the Basin of Tears, was placed at the doorway of the Old Barn. The Basin of Tears had existed for as long as anyone could remember, although no one would admit that they knew of such a place. Only shallow, happy thoughts were allowed in Harness. The names of the attendees were written on small pieces of paper and dropped in the jar. Trumpet blasts would then call everyone to the well, which was located in the center of the Old Barn. The well was covered with a green scum-like substance, which had to be skimmed off before each meeting. Eighteen feet across and a foot deep, the well wall was made of shale stone. A second trumpet blast brought the Elders to the raised platform overlooking the assembly. The Chief Elder would then randomly pick three names from the clay jar.

The first name drawn would be responsible for leading a singsong over the waters of the well. This was done in order to sweeten its bitterness. Remnants of the green scum that still lay on the surface should have disgusted the people, but they had experienced the film for so long that it was accepted as normal. Most of their teeth had long ago turned green.

The next name drawn was the Water-Giver. A golden ladle was handed down from the Chief Elder to the designated water-giver and each person would then be given a small drop of well water in a cup. The singsong did little to remove the bitterness of the water so a drop was all anyone desired.

The last name called was responsible for giving a closing benediction. It was by far the most awkward moment of the meeting as the poor unfortunate one who had been chosen was required to read a card that he had been given by the Elders. The sentiments read were typically the same week to week. Fancy flowery thanks to the Leaders of the flock were read in monotones that only a toad could appreciate.

Bisbee knew the rituals well. He could perform them in his sleep in such a meaningful way that no one would ever know they meant nothing to him.

Lost in his thoughts, Bisbee was startled by the first trumpet blast. The meeting was being called to order. Bisbee remained in the corner of the barn as friends and family filed past. Something began stirring inside of him. He had long ago lost interest in the meetings and had almost quit coming to them. The suffering that he and his fellow Harnessites were experiencing was relentless, and he was gradually coming to the conclusion that the meetings were, in some way, the cause of their distress.

The second blast of the trumpet brought everyone to their feet as The Elders entered and took their seats high above the well.

Bisbee watched as the Chief Elder reached into the clay jar, taking out one of the slips of paper.

"Mitch Miller."

Bisbee smiled from his hiding place. His friend had been chosen to lead the ceremonial singsong over the waters. Mitch hated to sing in public, and it was not because he could not sing. He actually sang quite well. Mitch hated the pressure he felt when he looked out at so many eyes watching his every move, and ears listening to his every note. He always sensed people were judging him, and it was enough to ruin every attempt he had ever made to perform. Watching Mitch in such torment had become quite enjoyable for Bisbee.

Mitch worked his way toward the front and positioned himself on the right side of the large round well. Joining hands, row by row, the assembly began swaying back and forth as Mitch began singing. What happened next can only be described as a case of extreme comedy, brought on by a purely random act of nature, in an unsuspecting crowd of people.

Mitch's bad notes and poorly timed transitions were interrupted by a red-breasted robin, which had flown in through an open door. Clearly agitated with the gathering, she dove in and out of the crowd until she finally hovered over the well and defecated into the waters. Mitch leapt into the well, attempting to contain the foreign object before it dissipated and ruined the singsong. Rising from his elevated chair, the Chief Elder directed the assembly to sing louder and sway harder. Bisbee was unable to control himself and fell from his perched position onto the barn floor. Laughing so hard his sides began to hurt, he attempted to regain his composure by joining in the singing, but it was of no use.

His laughter came to an abrupt end when he heard his name called from the Elder's chair.

"Bisbee Saxton."

His name had been drawn as the Water-Giver. The Chief Elder had risen from his chair and was staring at Bisbee as he lay on the barn floor. Standing to his feet, he wiped the tears from his eyes. Macafee's steely blue eyes cut deep. Brushing the hay off his pants, he swallowed hard and made his way to the well.

As he slowly worked through the crowd, he never took his eyes off the Elders. To look away for a moment would give the appearance of guilt, and Bisbee refused to allow them to condemn him for finding comedy in what was obviously a comical moment.

Mitch was climbing out of the water as Bisbee reached the well. Taking the golden ladle from Macafee, he turned to face the assembly. Looking into their faces he saw despair born of hopelessness. Bisbee counted row after row of thirsty, desperate people, who were longing for something, anything to satisfy their dry and dusty existence. He saw something more than just the torment of the Beasts. Bisbee saw a deep need for freedom from an unnamed enemy, a longing for something more than what he could dip out of the bitter well before him. They needed a supply of fresh water, not this green pond scum.

In that surreal moment everything became clear in Bisbee's mind. His suspicions concerning the meetings and the failure of the Elders to protect them from the Beasts could no longer be suppressed. With every eye fixed upon him, Bisbee made his decision, and he knew there was no turning back.

Bisbee stared into the stagnant waters before him and gripped the ladle tightly in his right hand. Raising his head, he looked into the eyes of Macafee. Panning the row of Elders, Bisbee met one set of condemning eyes after another.

Turning toward his old friend, Bisbee's face tensed. Mitch watched in disbelief as Bisbee recoiled and threw the sacred golden ladle into the far corner of the barn. A heavy silence choked the air as shock gave way to gasps. Bisbee fought through the crowd and finally broke out into the sunlight.

A quiet peace filled his soul. He knew he still did not have the answers he sought, but he was convinced he was headed in the right direction. His bridges were burning behind him with every step away from the Old Barn. He could not be a part of this charade any longer.

"Bisbee, wait up."

Mitch fought to catch his breath.

"You made a mess back there."

"I'm sorry, Mitch."

"Sorry for what? It's about time."

Bisbee looked up at his friend.

"Maybe you shouldn't be seen with me."

Mitch shook his head. "No, you don't understand. You should have seen what happened after you left."

"Maybe I don't want to know."

"You do."

Bisbee listened as Mitch explained how the people began to question the Elders concerning the water in the well. Tired of lacking a fresh drink, Bisbee had simply echoed the sentiments of all of Harness. He had been brave enough to stand against the Elders and refused to live any longer in fear.

"And the Elders? How did they respond?"

"They attacked you. They said you were a trouble-maker who just wanted to gain power over Harness."

"Maybe I am," responded Bisbee.

"We both know better than that."

As they came to a fork in the road, Mitch's breath became labored. Clutching his chest, he fell to the ground.

"Mitch, what's wrong?"

"It's my heart. It's beating too fast."

Sweat covered him as he groaned with intense pain. He struggled to get up but fell again.

"I'm going to get help."

Mitch grabbed his arm.

"There's something I haven't told you Bisbee."

"No, save your strength."

"You've got to hear this. The water in the well is too shallow. It stays contaminated all the time."

"How do you know," Bisbee asked.

"I tested it when the Elders weren't watching. The Beasts are ruining the water. The wells are being contaminated with their dung."

Bisbee thought about the warning in the cave. His mind flashed to all the wells, dotted across the countryside of Harness. Were they all contaminated?

"Find the answers, Bisbee. Don't give up until you discover the truth about the Beasts. It's killing all of us. Shallow wells, my friend, we're drinking out of shallow, contaminated wells."

Bisbee tried to leave but Mitch squeezed his arm even tighter.

"One more thing, Bisbee. They're riding them."

"Who is riding what?"

Mitch tried to answer but falling back to the ground he lost consciousness.

Bisbee stood up to get help, but when he did, the trees began to spin. Stumbling down the path he collapsed into a ditch.

The next thing Bisbee knew he was wiping the morning dew from his forehead. The rising sun was chasing the night darkness away as he opened his eyes. Staring into the water, he felt a soft kiss on his face. Avonlea was still sitting by his side holding his hand. Looking into her eyes, he saw tears flowing down her cheeks.

"Mitch was right, Bisbee. They were all shallow wells."

He squeezed her hand but when he did, she began to vanish before his eyes. Bisbee watched in sadness as an east wind slowly carried her image into the nearby field of clover.

In that moment, Bisbee realized the importance of his journey to Charis. He understood his freedom meant freedom to others. The questions plaguing him were the questions of every human heart. Bisbee was more determined than ever to discover the path to victory over the Beasts.

I love good preaching. It is exciting to sit under the ministry of a gifted speaker. Nothing is as inspiring as listening to the Word of Truth being rightly divided. The nourishment that we receive is life changing. However, it is possible to begin to depend too much on those times of "feeding." A concentration on the written word is no substitute for an abiding focus on Jesus, the Living Word. It is impossible to experience something while we are studying it, and in the midst of experiencing something, there is no time to study. Our study of the Bible must lead us to experience Jesus.

If we view the Bible as a book that gives life rather than one that points to the Life He has placed within us, then we have overstepped its intended purpose.[1] The valuable time that we spend reading, studying and listening to the Bible is meant to feed the Life that is already present. The daily experience of abiding in Jesus is meant to be one of constant rest. The Word of God does not increase the reality of His presence; it simply reminds us that He is always there.

The problem is simply this; sitting next to you in the pew is the elephant, and he is enjoying the preaching as much as you. The "big boy" refuses to move no matter what cranky church member comes along. His name is engraved on a gold plaque on the end cap. A loud "Amen," or a raised hand does not chase him off. The flesh is comfortable in a setting where Biblical knowledge is being substituted for God's life inside the believer. The elephant is happy to have your head filled with verses, as long as you keep them in your head. In Jesus' day, the Pharisees made the mistake of thinking that the Scriptures gave them life.[2]

I love worship. Music, which honors God, reminds us of His faithfulness and of His constant love for us. Powerful lyrics and beautiful arrangements help us to transcend our ordinary lives. Music offers a temporary reprieve from the struggles of daily living. To our delight, the flow of new worship music is as endless as a cornfield growing toward a distant horizon. What danger could there be in the cornfield of worship?

While enjoying beautiful melodies, it is easy to become dependent on the strings of an instrument to maintain a "right spirit." Like King Saul, our "evil spirit" is comforted by David's harp.[3] It is possible to embrace Christian music as a means of maintaining an upward swing in our walk with Christ. Enjoying verse and chorus, we believe that we have found a source of freedom, but it is a temporary "fix" at best.

As soon as we stop singing, we fall back into our spiritual funk and the dark clouds return. While driving down the road immersed in vehicular worship, a rude or careless driver cuts us off, choking us with anger. Turning the music up does not touch the rage we feel within. In fact, we usually turn the music off so that we can maintain our bad temper.

Worship music is a vital element of our Christian experience, but using it as a source of growth is like applying a bandage to a cancerous tumor. The flesh is at home in the "glory" brought on by a powerful performance on a church platform. The bull elephant plays a mean bass fiddle. What worship leader doesn't know the old joke; "Where did Satan land when he fell out of Heaven?" Answer: "The choir loft."

Music should never be a "hot-button" topic in our churches. If our attention is on the whether a drum-set should grace the stage, we are playing an unresolved chord. Fussing about music styles is a song for fools. The songs we sing are meant to vibrate the strings of the Life of Christ within us. As Edward Mote once wrote, "I dare not trust the sweetest frame, but wholly lean on Jesus' name."[4]

I love the joy of serving others. A careful examination of the early church reveals that it was a busy place. Feeding the widows, breaking bread from house to house, the Jerusalem assembly was a buzz of activity.[5] I remember being told early in my walk with Christ that I was "saved to serve," but does serving do anything to spur us along the path of growth? Is the elephant of our flesh quieted by our busyness in ministry?

It is easy to fall into the trap of thinking that if we bury ourselves in service, our own sinfulness will start to decay from starvation or neglect. This erroneous mindset assures us that if we just get busy helping others that our own self-centeredness will simply vanish into thin air. "Fixing" everyone else can be a comfortable place to hide when we ourselves are "broken."

Our attitude of ingratitude will disappear while handing a piece of bread to a homeless man. A prideful spirit will be washed down the sink, while serving in a soup kitchen. By signing up for "visitation" our negative spirits will shrink to munchkin size and wander away to a far country.

The great underlying issue of carnality is at home in the ministry of serving others. The beast hides behind the pots and pans. The flesh sneaks into the spice rack, seasoning everything we cook. We find ourselves filled with pride in serving others, critically questioning why others are not as involved.

Should we not be involved in ministry to our brothers and sisters in Christ? Yes, of course, but our deliverance from the power of sin is not found from signing up for every "opportunity" that the church provides for service.

As vital as these three areas are, they are powerless to liberate us from the carnality of our flesh. Preaching, singing, and service were never meant to deliver us. These ministries were given to us as a gift from Christ to express His life within the church. They were meant to glorify God.

In the Book of Acts, a detailed account is given regarding what happened on the day of Pentecost.[6] It is interesting to note what the Disciples were doing on that day or should I say what they were not doing.

The believers were gathered together in one accord. Peter was not preaching up a storm causing a thick cloud of conviction to hang over Jerusalem. James and John were not passing out loaves of bread to pilgrims as they entered the Temple, and Mary Magdalene was not leading the group in songs of praise.

To be completely honest with the Scripture, the disciples in the Upper Room were simply waiting. Take a few moments and allow the whole concept of waiting to sink into your mind.

The church was not scrambling to schedule a revival or readjusting programs to suit whatever they believed would net and keep the most fish. There was no activity on the part of the Disciples in the upper room that caused heaven to move. They were waiting on their Lord. There was no plan "B" in the works. If the Holy Spirit did not show up, then the church would just continue to wait. The church is an organism, with Christ being her nucleus.

The life of Christ, as it resides in the soul of man, is like an artesian well. In contrast, religion offers us detailed instructions in the art of well digging, complete with a shovel. We are then encouraged to dig our own water supply and find our sustenance by grit and gravel. Can you honestly say that your ceaseless efforts to produce spirituality have resulted in anything other than religious fatigue? Jesus promised that His yoke was easy and His burden was light.[7] Has your road become light and easy by following the mandates of religion? Have you found rest for your soul in the multiplicity of church activities?

The water that these man-made wells provide barely resembles the flowing fountain of His Life in us. These religious run-offs need our constant maintenance. The springs of Christ flow naturally requiring nothing but a cup. The abiding victory we seek is never drawn from wells of our own digging. Any efforts on our part to grow spiritually resemble shallow wells.

The local church can become a hindrance if we think of her as the path to victory. There is a strong temptation to believe that the church is the source of spirituality rather than the expression of it. Our lungs use the oxygen we take in, but they are not the origin of it.

The consideration before us is not whether ministry is important. Certainly there is great value in being involved in the local church. Without any question, we should sit under sound Biblical preaching, we should sing the Songs of Zion and we should be involved in service to others.

The overflowing artesian well of His Life in us does not need to be supported by any human endeavor. The root of a tree produces the fruit on the branches not the other way around.[8]

Ministry should be the overflow of His Life, not the means to it. We are more than conquerors but not by anything we do in the church. Shallow wells are tempting, but they always leave a bitter taste and a dry soul.

CHAPTER 12

WALNUTS & BOVINE

Staring into the clover, Bisbee wondered if Avonlea could ever forgive him. He had kept her in Harness far too long. She had tried to tell him that there was a better life outside of Harness, but he had refused to listen. How had he not seen the shallowness of it all?

Marnin must have had a reason to leave him in Harness. Following the Master was, at times, puzzling. He had always granted Bisbee the freedom to make his own decisions, and yet Marnin seemed to stand in the shadow, somehow guiding the whole process. Marnin never forced his will on those who chose to follow him. How could he allow the Elders to continue year after year in the ignorance of bondage? Or were they ignorant? Maybe when the last piece of the puzzle was snapped into place, he would understand Harness.

Hearing a familiar voice call from across the stream, Bisbee looked up. On the west bank sat Marnin, feet hanging in the water and a fishing pole in his right hand. The Master looked in Bisbee's direction.

"Not much biting today. When there's a full moon, it'll be better fishing."

Bisbee wondered if he had been there all along. Marnin smiled. In the midst of his saddened heart, Bisbee smiled back. The Master always had a way of cheering him up.

"So, what have you learned, my friend?"

Bisbee pulled a tall stalk of grass from the creek bank and began bending it between his fingers. He had experienced so much since entering Charis, and he knew the importance of Marnin's question. The mysteries of the Well of Chayah would mean nothing to him unless he was ready to receive them. After rolling over in his mind all he had seen and heard, Bisbee finally spoke.

"I've learned that the air in Charis is cleaner and lighter than the heavy air of Harness. I understand that I am no match for the strength of the Beast. As much as I hate the thought, I know the Beast is somehow attached to me. I've discovered that there are enemies who oppose Charis, and that they will lie in order to bring them back to Harness."

Picking up a small flat stone, Bisbee skipped it down the length of the stream. Watching the round ripples float slowly to the banks, he continued.

"I think I understand the People of Glassy Pond. They believe that they are part of Charis but they are not. They view the land as a place designed for their own pleasure and fulfillment."

Bisbee looked back up the hill and into the Wood. He was thankful to be free from its enchantments.

Marnin looked at the Traveler with kindness.

"I understand Harness is a land of empty promises. It is a culture created by men attempting to shelter its followers from the reality of the Beasts. The Meeting Place is a house of ignorance and their well is shallow and contaminated."

"What about the map and the writings?" Marnin asked.

Bisbee reached into his pocket.

"I'll never be without them again. I've learned that the opinions of men are useless compared to what you have written."

A soft smile broke on the Master's face, and his eyes danced with delight.

"You're almost ready, Bisbee. Charlie is waiting for you at the black walnut tree."

"Almost?"

"You have a few more stops on the way. There are no short cuts to the Well of Chayah, Bisbee. Keep the writings and the map close to you and read them very carefully. The closer you get to the Well, the greater the danger."

Marnin stood up and began walking across the field toward Broken Dam. Bisbee began to call after him, but he knew it was of no use. Once Marnin walked away, he was finished with the moment. He had given all the information that was necessary for his next step. What danger was Marnin speaking of? Had he not faced enough foes and survived his share of drama?

Tucking the map and the writings safely underneath his right arm, Bisbee headed south toward the bridge. The morning sun had finally succeeded in burning off the fog, and the Traveler was happy to be on his way again. Passing by one of Hugabone's rusty traps, he found a stick and stuck it in the pan. The spring recoiled and the jaws snapped the stick in two. Bisbee wondered what could have happened to cause Hugabone to be so cruel. Perhaps the old trapper secretly desired to enter Charis but could not overcome his fear of the Elders. Passing over to the west bank, he determined to never again venture out of Charis.

True to Marnin's word, Charlie was under the walnut tree. He was holding something in his right hand, and he appeared to be mumbling to himself. Bisbee watched as Charlie slammed the object again and again onto an exposed tree root. Amused with the muskrat's apparent frustration, Bisbee began to laugh.

"What are you doing?"

Charlie detected the sarcasm in Bisbee's voice but decided to ignore it. Turning away, he slammed the object down once again, this time badly bruising his knuckles.

"Ever tried to crack a fresh walnut?"

"No, you're supposed to wait until they dry up at bit."

"Well, I like them fresh. If you wait until they're dry, they get stuck in your teeth, and I don't want something stuck in these pearly whites."

The muskrat grinned ear to ear. Bisbee was uncertain as to whether Charlie's proud display of magnificent molars was a show of conceit or an offering of humble gratitude to his Maker. The determined muskrat again raised his hand and brought the shell down hard onto the root. Successful, Charlie sat enjoying his snack. He smiled again:

"See? Nothing in my teeth."

"Don't you think we should be on our way?" Bisbee asked.

"Bisbee, Bisbee, always in a hurry. Have you ever thought of slowing down to enjoy the scenery? Taking time to smell the cracked walnuts of life?"

Bisbee was irritated by Charlie's apparent lack of urgency. Sitting there at the base of the Walnut Tree was Bisbee's guide; he was secure and true no matter how petulant. Bisbee knew that he could get to the Well between the map and the writings, but he felt that without Charlie the journey may not be as enlightening.

"Sit down."

Charlie handed Bisbee a walnut. Leaning his head against the tree, Bisbee tried not to look agitated. Charlie tossed his shells to the ground, ignoring his friend's bad mood.

"Look at those cows, Bisbee. What are they doing?"

Bisbee glanced into the field.

"Oh let me see, chewing their cud?"

"Do you know what a cud consists of?"

Bisbee smiled.

"It's regurgitated food," he responded.

"So it is. The hay that a cow first chews is raw. After he swallows it must be "brought up" again and again before it is ever ready to be properly digested. The key my friend, is slow digestion. If you don't slow down and chew, you'll end up with a stomach ache."

Closing his eyes, Bisbee leaned his head back against the tree trunk. The Traveler quietly chewed on Charlie's last statement. Opening his eyes, he looked back at the cows. Saliva pouring out of their mouths, jaws flexing back and forth, the cows worked their cud relentlessly. The bovine in the field slowly chewed their food, refusing to swallow for a last time until it was soft.

The Traveler had been exposed to so much that was new to him, and his stomach did hurt a little. He decided to be more patient with himself. No short cuts, no quick fixes and no need to understand everything that he was experiencing. Like the splitting of the clouds to reveal the sun, all would be clear in time.

He looked over at Charlie and smiled. The muskrat started up the trail toward the farmhouse, satisfied that Bisbee had gotten the point.

"What are you going to do with your walnut?" Charlie called back to Bisbee.

"I'll wait till it dries out a bit."

CHAPTER 13

THE FOREST OF SHEDAR

Charlie walked directly to the machine shed after passing the Red Barn. He climbed up on a rusty oil drum and peered in through a broken window.

"Come on, where is she?" the muskrat muttered to himself.

"Who."

Charlie craned his neck and looked back at Bisbee.

"Beatrice."

"Who." Agitated, the muskrat again turned towards Bisbee.

"The owl." Charlie responded.

"Whoo."

The muskrat was on the verge of giving Bisbee a piece of his mind, that he could ill afford to lose, when the Traveler pointed above him.

Bisbee whispered, "She's on the roof."

Suddenly, the huge bird flew past Charlie, causing the muskrat to lose his balance and fall back into a stack of old tractor tires. Beatrice landed only a few feet from Bisbee. As Charlie attempted to free himself from the black rubber maze of tires, the owl turned toward Bisbee.

"He's very clumsy, you know. I mean Charlie, of course. You would think a muskrat would be more agile but not that one. Whenever I get bored, I go down to Living Stream and watch him try to catch fish. It's quite a show. I never let him know I'm watching. It would hurt his feelings."

Bisbee stepped back to get a better look at Beatrice. Standing with perfect posture, her face was snowy white with a heart shaped ring around its perimeter. Her soft white chest was covered with small, black dots that begged to be connected, yet the tiny specks were so randomly placed that any attempt was doomed to fail. The owl's wings were her most spectacular feature. Rustic brown with hints of charcoal black, they were an artist's dream. As Bisbee looked her over, the only word that came to his mind was "magnificent."

Beatrice the Owl

Charlie, having recovered himself from the tire pile, looked up to see Bisbee and Beatrice staring at him. Eager to be rid of an embarrassing moment, he spoke quickly.

"Well, it looks as though you two will get along just fine. I'll be on my way."

"Where are you going?"

"You're in good hands, Bisbee. Beatrice knows the way. I'll meet you at the Well."

Charlie called to the collie dog, which was standing in the cellar doorway of the farmhouse. Together they walked toward Broken Dam. Bisbee turned to ask Beatrice a question, but the owl had already begun walking up the gravel driveway next to the farmhouse. Caught off guard by the fast moving owl, Bisbee ran to catch up.

Pausing to take a rest, the Traveler spotted the Rhubarb patch and the beehive that he had seen the week before, as he sat with Marnin on Ascending Hill. The beehive was buzzing wildly from some sort of movement on the porch. Bisbee tried to see the Well, but it was hidden under the apple tree.

"Are you coming?"

Beatrice had reached the midpoint of the driveway and was looking impatiently back at Bisbee. The Traveler pointed across the backyard.

"The Well is over there. Shouldn't we be headed in that direction?"

Beatrice said nothing. Patience was not one of the owl's virtues. She also possessed a certain affinity for being on time, and Bisbee was making her late. She folded her wings by her sides and began tapping her foot at a rate of speed that made him dizzy. Her large, green eyes narrowed, which caused Bisbee to look away. The Traveler dropped his head. What difference did it make which *side of the house they went around? Perhaps he should trust his feathered friend. Marnin had warned of shortcuts. Bisbee joined Beatrice and together they walked up the drive.*

The Traveler was anxious about being this close to the Well of Chayah. The Master had spoken of a final test, which included a certain temptation. Nothing could hinder him now that he was so close to the Well!

Deep in thought, Bisbee did not notice that a thick black fog was descending from above. Within seconds, the fog had blanketed the entire area. The Traveler found himself struggling to find his way. The sound of gravel under his feet was his only reassurance that he was still on the driveway. Turning to ask Beatrice for help, he realized that she was gone. Bisbee knew that it was useless trying to find the owl in the black cloud. Suddenly, the sound of huge wings passed by, and Bisbee found himself at the edge of a dense forest. The smell of damp birch trees filled the air, as a distant sound began to find its way into Bisbee's ears.

At first, it sounded like the muffled cry of a bobcat, but as Bisbee stepped into the forest, the cries gave way to a furious war chant. The terrifying screams were like nothing Bisbee had ever heard. His first response was to run, but then he heard what he thought to be a familiar voice. The advance halted, and he heard the voice again. Could it be his son, Stephen?

Bisbee crouched behind a huge oak tree and contemplated his next move. Should he remain hidden or call out to the war party? Nothing could have prepared him for what he was about to experience.

A thunderous roar sent Bisbee to the ground. A Crimson Bull elephant had emerged out of the fog and was running for its life. As the Beast turned to face its attackers, blood poured from its head and shoulders. Rearing back on its hind legs, its eyes were bulging with fury. The Beast bellowed again. A flaming spear cut through the fog, landing just below its midsection. The cries of the warriors grew louder. Another spear flew from the dense mist, striking the Beast directly in the chest. A sickening cry filled the air as the elephant crashed to the ground.

The blood-soaked Beast lay motionless against a huge maple tree. As the victorious cries of the warriors faded in the distance, Bisbee came out from behind the oak tree and slowly approached, listening for the breath of the elephant. The Red Bull lay in dead stillness. All that the Traveler could hear was the sound of his own breathing. Leaning in closer to the Beast, Bisbee reached out his hand to touch it. The blood from its wounds soaked Bisbee's shoes.

Without warning, the creature opened a blood-shot eye, sending Bisbee backward onto the ground. The Beast climbed to its feet and after lowering its head, turned toward Bisbee. The elephant began spitting green phlegm into Bisbee's face as it pawed the ground.

Suddenly, Bisbee heard the sound of wings. Beatrice had flown past him and landed between him and the Red Beast. Raising her feathers high, she began to quake. With her head lifted high, the owl let out a deafening scream. Bisbee watched in amazement as the terrified Beast turned and ran down the trail, disappearing into the dark forest. Overcome with fear and exhaustion, Bisbee fell to the ground.

When the Traveler came to, he stood up and braced himself against a tree. The fog had finally lifted, and Bisbee was able to see the field of battle. He was shocked to see damaged tree trunks covered with blood, muddy terrain dug up by fierce combat, and weapons lying on the ground. Scattered over the battlefield were bits and pieces of Marnin's writings. Beatrice was about to speak when Bisbee saw someone walking toward them.

"Stephen? Is that you?"

Bisbee ran to embrace his son. He could see in Stephen's eyes an excitement mixed with weariness. Bisbee heard the sound of wings from high in the tree cover, and after watching Beatrice fly off into the distance, Bisbee turned back toward his son.

"Stephen, are you alright? What are you doing here? I thought you were back in Harness leading the rebellion."

"The rebellion is over. MacAfee is dead. It was a fungus of some kind that killed him. Most of the people of Harness are on their way to Charis. I've come ahead."

Bisbee looked under his son's ear, trying to see if the fungus was still there. Stephen turned away.

"Stephen, is your mother among those that are coming to Charis?"

His son smiled.

"Of course she is. She can't wait to see you."

"But why are you here? What are you doing in the Forest of Shedar?" Bisbee asked.

The young man looked confused.

"Fighting, of course. The warriors of the Tribe of Gibbor met me on the way. I thought I'd find you with them."

With great excitement, Stephen told his father of the Tribe of Gibbor and the conquests of The Forest of Shedar. The history of the tribe fascinated Bisbee. These ancient warriors had spanned generations, recruiting new warriors from lands like Harness. Committed to the destruction of the Beasts, they battled with weapons forged in the Valley of Sinai. Bisbee saw weariness in Stephen's eyes, but he knew his son would never admit to such a thing, so he decided to keep quiet.

"Father, these warriors are men of valor. They are elite fighters for the cause of Marnin's honor."

Bisbee wondered why Marnin had not told him of these men. Stephen showed his father the iron weapons of Gibbor. They seemed too heavy for warfare, but the blood dripping from the trees seemed to tell another story. Bisbee picked up a torn piece of Marnin's writings.

"Stephen, why are these here?"

"We wage our battles according to the writings. Pages are torn out to make it easier to carry them into the fight. Father, this is a great war, and it is the way into Charis."

As the words rolled off of Stephen's lips, Marnin's warning shot deep into Bisbee heart: "The only way into Charis is Crossing Bridge." Had his son been deceived?

Bisbee quietly listened as Stephen recounted the exploits of the Tribe of Gibbor. Nothing would bring Bisbee greater joy than to kill the Beasts with his own hands, but he knew that this was not the path into Charis. The battles in Harness were never like what he had just witnessed, and yet did these warriors really believe that they could defeat these unstoppable devils of destruction? The elephant had recovered so quickly from what appeared to have been a mortal wound. Bisbee knew that the weapons of Sinai would never bring down the enemy, but he also knew that the intoxicating thrill of fighting these Beasts was a hard thing to walk away from.

"Stephen, listen to me. There is only one way into Charis, and it is Crossing Bridge. The map and the writings are very clear. If you would just slow down long enough to read them, you would see it. Marnin has already provided the way. All this fighting is unnecessary."

"Oh yes, the easy way!" responded Stephen.

"What are you talking about? Marnin built Crossing Bridge. How can you call it the 'easy way'?"

Stephen's lips tightened.

"There is no conquest without struggle and no crown without a fight. Father, our destiny is to enter the Land of Charis. You know this. You are the one who challenged the people in Harness. Our people are on their way as we speak. What will they find in their leader when they arrive? A warrior who battles against the Beasts or a man who takes the easy way? If we defeat the Beasts now, then a full entrance will be opened into Charis for all our people."

Stephen had always possessed the ability to persuade others in a cause. Bisbee admired his passion. A sense of responsibility began to pull at Bisbee. What would the people find in him when they arrived? Taking the fight directly to the enemy began to make better sense then to wander aimlessly toward an old, moss-covered well. What victory could there be in the shade of an apple tree? There was no crowd of people flocking around the Well of Chayah. Stephen sensed his struggle.

"Father, come with us. Together we'll please Marnin. Side by side we'll enjoy great victories over the Beasts."

Bisbee looked over Stephen's shoulder into a tangled mess of broken branches and muddy terrain. The forest with its smell of blood and promise of warfare had excited him. Marnin had done so much for him. Fighting for the Master's honor seemed to be a small price to pay. The desire to battle alongside his son against the creatures who had brought such misery was strong. Crossing Bridge began to feel too easy.

"Father, are you listening to me? The Tribe needs a man like you."

Bisbee looked down to where the elephant had fallen. Its blood was slowly drying on his shoes. Bisbee missed the feelings of importance he had experienced in Harness. The desire to join his son was intense. Perhaps he could someday lead this Tribe of Gibbor. He bent over to pick up the spear that had pierced the Beast. As he struggled to lift the heavy weapon, the sound of wings caused Bisbee to lower his head. Dropping the spear at Stephen's feet, Bisbee looked up and saw Beatrice perched on the limb of a quaking aspen. The wise owl sat silently on her lofty branch.

Had he been through so much and learned so little? The words of Marnin had been so clear. Was he ready to abandon his journey to the Well of Chayah for the empty promise of killing a Beast that he had just seen recover from death? Looking into the eyes of Beatrice, Bisbee knew that he had once again begun to follow his own heart instead of Marnin. He understood why the wisdom of the Master appeared foolish to the Tribe of Gibbor. They would rather fight than simply follow.

How could he have devalued the bridge that Marnin had built, as if it were a cheap and easy way into Charis? Bisbee felt a deep shame. The Master had built Crossing Bridge with his own hands. The thought almost brought Bisbee to tears.

"No Stephen, I can't go with you."

"They told me you'd say that." Stephen crossed his arms.

"Who?"

"The Elders of Gibbor. They said you'd want the easy way, the lazy path. They told me you would twist the writings of Marnin."

Stephen turned to walk away. Bisbee reached out and grabbed his arm.

"Let go of me. You're a coward!"

"No, Stephen. I watched the Beast die right here where we're standing. He came back to life. You've got to listen. These creatures cannot be killed with your weapons. Wound them all you want, they recover."

Bisbee released his arm and softened his voice.

"The answers we seek are found in The Well of Chayah in the Land of Charis. Come with me. I'll take you to Crossing Bridge. The entrance into the land is not through the Forest of Shedar. I don't yet understand it all Stephen, but I do know there are answers at the Well. Marnin has made that very clear."

The two men stood together under the cover of the forest looking into each other's eyes. The sound of the Warriors of Gibbor grew faint in the distance. Stephen looked off in their direction. Turning back to Bisbee, his face became hardened.

"We follow the writings of Marnin. If the Beasts cannot be killed, then what difference does it make? At least we are doing something for the cause. We are fighting. You're doing nothing!"

"Don't you see what the Tribe is doing? They tear out the parts of the writings that they want to use for their futile campaigns against the Beasts. The writings were meant to be studied as a whole. You'll never find the way to true victory from a map that's been torn apart."

Steven turned away, refusing to listen.

Bisbee's heart broke into a thousand pieces. Would he ever be able to convince his son that fighting in Shedar was rejecting Marnin's offer of true victory? Stephen was turning away from the wisdom of Marnin. His son was so close to Charis and yet so far from Crossing Bridge. The Tribe of Gibbor possessed the writings but only carried bits and pieces of them into battle. They were destined to fail. These warriors appealed to Stephen's sense of valor, and Bisbee saw he would not be persuaded. Looking into the eyes of his son, he made one last attempt.

"Stephen, I want you to think about something. If you could kill the Beasts, how many would you have to defeat to enter Charis? At what point would the blood of these Beasts give way to ultimate victory? If Marnin's writings speak of full victory at the Well, why are you wasting your time in this Forest? There is only one entrance into the Land, and it is the Bridge that Marnin has built."

Stephen's eyes filled with tears. Taking a step closer to his father, he laid his weapon down. Bisbee saw the weariness written in deep lines across the young man's face. He had been in the Forest for such a short time, and yet, it had taken its toll on him. Bisbee reached out to embrace his son but Stephen stepped back.

"I'm sorry, father."

Picking up his spear, Stephen turned back toward the thick forest. The two men exchanged a look of sadness that neither one of them could have anticipated. A hidden fork in the road had led both men to choose two very different paths, and at least for now, there was no turning back. By blood they would always be close, but by spirit they had been torn apart.

The roar of an elephant in the distance severed the moment. Stephen turned and ran into the forest as Bisbee looked up to see Beatrice still sitting in the aspen. Spreading her wings, she flew in the direction of Charis. With a heavy and yet peaceful heart, Bisbee followed.

Spiritual warfare is real. The flesh, the world and the Devil all oppose those who follow Christ.[1] To deny that we live in a spiritual war-zone is to live in a fool's paradise. It is akin to setting up a picnic on a battlefield. By choosing Christ, we have chosen to swim against the current. The question is not whether there is conflict; rather, it is if we are engaged in the fight and what are the weapons of our warfare?

In the Book of Ephesians, the Christian is commanded to first rest in the position that God has placed him.[2] He is then told to walk worthy of this seated position in Christ.[3] Then and only then, the soldier of Christ is commanded to stand against the schemes of the devil.[4] He did not command the Christian to march or to fight: the believer is told to "stand." Christ does not give us victory; He is our victory.

We yield the high ground of established victory and enter the forest of struggle when we choose to use our methods and strategies in the fight against sin. When we look to ourselves, we take our eyes off of the Master. We cry out for His help, but no aid is given because we are choosing to fight a battle in a war that is already won.

As a young boy, I once walked past a herd of cows grazing in a pasture. A large black bull stood in the midst of the bovine. As I walked down the dirt road, the bull followed my every movement. A four-foot barbwire fence separated us. Feelings of youthful invincibility overcame me, and I jumped the fence. With each step toward the beast my anxiety grew. Suddenly the bull lowered his head and began charging. I retreated at full sprint, leaping over the fence just in time. Covered with dirt and grass, I spun around and faced the raging beast. Standing face to face, with nothing more than a wire fence between us, he made his position on the matter of my entering his field quite clear. I never again ventured into the bull's domain.

If we adopt a mentality of "methods" for victory, we are actually fighting on the enemy's terms and conditions. We enter the field of the bull. Countering the Devil's schemes, we attempt "schemes" of our own. We may gain partial victories but at the end of the day, the bull always wins. Beaten and bloody, we dive over a four-foot wire fence and discover that we have underestimated our foe.

In contrast to the "schemes" of the devil, we are to put on the whole "armor of God".[5] This is not armor that has been given to us from God: it is God Himself who is our armor. It is in the strength of His might, not ours, that we conquer. As the power of Christ rests upon us, we enjoy victory.[6] It is Christ that makes the difference. In spite of all this, we still choose to take on the bull.

Our human reasoning cries out for a plan of action. We crave being a part of the process. Engaging in seasons of prayer and fasting in order to gain victory is our method. Renewing our pledge of faithfulness to the Lord sounds like the right thing to do. It appeals to our sense of valor. It just makes sense to do something rather than nothing; however, is looking to the Lord for victory really an exercise in spiritual laziness?

To be very clear at this point, anything we "do" to gain victory over our sinful tendencies is a method or strategy. A dedication of our efforts in any form is a weapon that is too heavy to carry into the fight. Calls to action or a pledge of loyalty are both doomed to fail. Consider the following statements:

"I'll stop listening to…"

"I will stop going there…"

"I'll begin to do this…"

"I will dedicate my life in a deeper way to the Lord."

"Lord, I need your help with my attitude."

All these statements include something we are going to "do" to defeat sin. Our commitment to conquer sin may be as sincere as Peter's pledge of loyalty on the night Jesus was crucified.[7] The crow of the rooster sent Peter to the "weeping room." That same rooster is still crowing today, highlighting our failed attempts to gain advantage over sin by our methods. We can do nothing to bring victory over sin: it is His life in us that matters.

Herein lies the rub, the question that divides those who walk in victory and those who fall. Does He give us power for victory over the flesh or is He the victory?

Does Christ come alongside the believer, filling him with power, or has the Lord Himself already won the victory? Do I activate His power in me as a result of prescribed disciplines, or is His power always present in me based on His redemptive work? Is it "Christ and me" or "Christ in me?" That is the key. The difference between the two viewpoints is bigger than you might think.

There is only one path that God has given us to live in constant victory. As Jesus was dying on the cross, He cried out, "It is finished." In His shout of victory, Satan was defeated and the reign of sin was over. His triumph was complete and sin itself was conquered. From the divine perspective, the war was won and as a result of His victory, He gained and continues to hold the upper hand. The present spiritual battle rages on, but our fight is against a defeated foe. It is "Christ in me," that wins the day.[8]

God is the Author and Finisher of our faith.[9] He is the Author in that He first gave us the gift of faith when we got saved. He is the Finisher as He continues to grow us by faith. No effort was exerted on our part when we came to Christ, and no effort is to be offered on our part in growth. Paul asks the question, "Having begun in the Spirit, are you now made perfect by the flesh?"[10] Christ did not help us get saved;

He saved us! He has no intention of helping us gain victory. He is our victory! The Forest of Shedar is a place of bondage.

We are told to fight the good fight of faith; yet, there is to be no effort on our part in the battle against sin.[11] The entire struggle took place on the Cross of Christ. The flesh, the Devil and the world were crushed by His triumph. When we rest in this truth, the victory is always ours. But how is this accomplished in our lives in a practical way?

When crossing the Red Sea, Moses was told to "stand firm and see the salvation of the Lord."[12] The Psalms declare, "Be still and know that I am God."[13] We are more than conquerors through Him who loved us.[14] He does not command us to conquer; He declares that we are already victorious.

The thrill of hunting the beasts deafens the call to come to the mystery of the Well of Chayah. The warriors in the Forest of Shedar boast of impressive numbers. In contrast, the Well is much less populated. To compound the problem, confusion abounds, and misinformation is common concerning this place of victory. Those who are busy fighting in the Forest, discredit the Well, citing the lack of effort it takes to simply "free fall."

The methods of men just lead us deeper into the forest of despair. A wounded, bleeding elephant may give temporal relief and a sense of accomplishment, but the beast will rise again. He is perfectly content for you to continue working your "strategies" in an attempt to defeat him.

God's ultimate victory in our lives is not found in the Forest of Shedar. By our struggling against sin we only sink deeper into it. The loud bellowing and the gathering dung pile of the beast should be all the proof that we need.

CHAPTER 14

THE CAVE OF SPIT-YAK

Bisbee discovered a grassy trail leading in the direction that Beatrice had flown. With every step down the path, Bisbee was walking away from his first-born. The memories of Stephen's blood, pouring off their kitchen table from a wound inflicted by the Beasts, flooded Bisbee's mind. Would he have to watch him bleed again? Perhaps this time he would have to kiss his son goodbye.

The blade that separated them was sharper than the memories of that fateful night. His son was blindly following a tribe of warriors, hunting Beasts that were indestructible, and Bisbee was powerless to stop him. Stephen had always displayed a deep respect for his father; yet, now he had chosen nameless warriors over his father's pleadings. Bisbee racked his brain for some way to rescue Stephen, but every path of possible rescue led to a murky swamp. The Traveler came to the painful conclusion that he was helpless to rescue him from Shedar. He could only hope that his son's failures in the forest would someday help him see the truth of Crossing Bridge.

Teary-eyed, Bisbee abandoned thoughts of visiting Stephen; he knew that it would only make matters worse. The savory taste of battle would be difficult for the young warrior to get out of his mouth. His son would have to discover the truth on his own. Leaving him in Shedar, and returning to the Land of Charis was the only way. They would always be family, but at this time, their spirits were a million miles apart. A coarse dryness filled Bisbee's throat.

The Traveler was surprised at how long it was taking him to reach the edge of the Forest. Only a few steps had brought Bisbee into Shedar, but the journey out seemed endless. Perhaps he needed the long walk to rid his mind of the Forest.

He was sure by now Beatrice had returned to Charis and was updating Charlie on what had transpired in the Forest.

As night descended, Bisbee searched for the border of Charis. He tried to press on, but the shadowy dusk was making it difficult to stay on the trail. Loneliness hung like a thick cloud around Bisbee's heart. The sound of thunder in the distance convinced him to seek shelter for the night. Bisbee discovered a cave opening in the side of a hill, and after entering the underground cavern, he found a small pile of oak wood. The cave floor was littered with torn pages from Marnin's writings. The warriors of Gibbor must have used this rock fortress for a meeting place.

After starting a small fire, the weary Traveler found a smooth place in the rocks across from the burning oak and sat down. The warmth of the fire felt good to his cold and battered face. Pulling a piece of dried meat from his satchel, he wondered what Stephen was eating tonight. How he missed his son. What would he say to Avonlea when she arrived? He found himself longing for his wife. Perhaps tomorrow he would see Avonlea and the others at the bridge.

His thoughts were interrupted by the sound of beating rain against the mouth of the cave. The promised storm had arrived, and Bisbee was thankful to be in a dry place. Leaning back against the damp limestone wall, Bisbee reached into his pocket and felt the black walnut that Charlie had given him earlier. He smiled.

"This must be my chewing time," Bisbee muttered to himself.

Happy to be past his last hurdle, Bisbee began to relax and took a moment to acclimate himself to his surroundings. As he closed his eyes, he enjoyed the musty smell of the cave. The sound of running water from a nearby stream reminded him of Crossing Bridge. Bisbee hoped to see Charlie again, but he knew it was Marnin's face that would soothe his aching heart.

Falling in and out of sleep, the Traveler spent his waking moments trying to get comfortable on the rugged rocks. A brown bat occasionally flew past, jarring him awake. The experiences of the last few days visited Bisbee in dreams, and at one point he thought he heard movement in the cave. Thinking it was Stephen; he arose and searched its passageways until he was too tired to continue. Still a little uneasy, Bisbee lay back down and soon fell into a deep sleep.

At midnight he was awakened by a smell so repulsive that he immediately recoiled. The rain had stopped and was replaced by a cold wind sweeping through the entrance of the cave. The chilling breeze did nothing to dispel the sickening scent hanging in the air; rather, it seemed to accentuate the odor. The Traveler noticed his ankle beginning to throb.

The fire was dying but enough of the burning embers remained to illuminate a figure sitting directly across from Bisbee. It was holding something in its left hand. The figure drew long labored breaths in unnatural intervals. A low, gurgling sound accompanied each breath, as if it were strangling on something. Its head was covered with a thick black, woolen hood.

Bisbee doubled over from nausea and spewed against the cave wall. With watery eyes he stared into the vomit and realized that he had smelled the stench before, but where? And then he remembered. It was the day that he had seen the creature in Coopers Cave.

"Could it be Spit-Yak?" he asked himself.

Turning toward the cavern entrance, his first impulse was to run, but he had no idea how fast or powerful this thing was. Bisbee backed up closer to the cave wall and attempted to calmly calculate his next move. Where was Marnin?

The Traveler and the creature sat across from each other in heavy silence. The creature began swaying back and forth, and then suddenly it stopped. With a voice like a thousand hardened fingernails sliding down a cracked chalkboard, it spoke.

"Did you sssmell the blood in the Forest today?"

As he lifted his eyes toward the demon, Bisbee's heart pounded wildly. A long, jagged scar ran from its left ear, along the length of its jaw, and back around its neck. A steady flow of yellow mucus dripped from the corner of its mouth down onto its swollen stomach. When it spoke, Bisbee could smell a putrefying odor coming from its inward parts. Scaly skin followed swollen cheek lines to the bridge of its nose. Its eyes were glazed over with a thick, crimson substance. The creature was looking down at Bisbee's feet.

"You have blood on your shoes."

Unable to move, the Traveler watched in horror as the creature extended its long split tongue and began to lick the dried blood from Bisbee's left shoe. Retracting its tongue, the demon's eyes dilated. A twisted expression spread across its face as it began to slowly sway back and forth.

"You know who I am, don't you? The rodent told you my name."

Bisbee slowly nodded. He now wished that Charlie had not spoken the demon's name. Spit-Yak continued.

"There are many like me who were wise enough to rebel against the tyranny of the Oppressor years ago. We are waiting for the great day of glory when the master will defeat the Oppressor."

The creature curled up next to Bisbee and hissed.

"I was asssigned to you on the day that you foolishly decided to follow the Great Liar. I know all about you. I was there when Marnin wasn't. I've watched your every move for years, and as surprising as it might sound, I've grown quite fond of you."

Bisbee recoiled as the creature slid closer to him.

"What is that condescending look, Bisbee? Do I appear hideous to you? I'm no more disgusting than the Beast that connects us. He's yours, you know."

Bisbee recalled the confrontation under the black walnut tree. He knew that the Beast was his, but was he also connected to Spit-Yak because of the Beast? The Traveler had heard enough.

Bisbee attempted to flee, but the creature quickly blocked his path.

"Not so fast, my friend. We have much to talk about. We share many fond memoriesss, that need to be mutually enjoyed."

Crawling back to the fire, the Traveler could only stare hopelessly at the creature sitting before him.

"Do you really think he cares for you?"

"Who?"

"The Evil One."

"Do you mean Marnin?"

At the mention of Marnin's name the creature shrieked. Slamming up against the cave wall, it shook with violent convulsions. Shocked at Spit-Yak's sudden reaction, Bisbee watched with great fascination. He had never realized that Marnin's name carried such power. After recovering itself, the creature leaned in toward Bisbee.

"He cares for you as long as you obey his commands. He is making you his slave, which is all you will ever be to him. The moment you turn away from him, he will turn away from you. Look at my face Bisbee. This is a result of rejecting the one you think is so wonderful. Has he promised you freedom? It's a lie."

Bisbee felt in the darkness for the writings.

Spit-Yak snarled, "You are nothing but a puppet on a string to amuse the Great Impostor."

Remembering that the writings were near the fire, Bisbee reached for them. He quickly unfolded the document, but the darkness of the cave was too great, and the fire was too small for Bisbee to make out the words. Spit-Yak leaned in so close that Bisbee could smell the creature's hideous breath. Cold green mucus dripped from the demon's mouth onto Bisbee forearm. Once again fighting back the urge to vomit, the Traveler began to tremble. The clouds that had covered the night sky cleared to reveal a full moon at the entrance of the cave. Light broke in as Bisbee looked down at Marnin's writings. Softly, he read from the open page.

"You are my great delight. I dance over you with overflowing joy. Nothing can ever separate you from my great love."

Spit-Yak's body jerked against the cave wall as its head slammed into a jagged rock. Blood ran down the side of its face as it snarled at the moon. The clouds returned, and once again darkness filled the cave. As the creature paced back and forth, its breathing grew more laborious. Glowing, red eyes searched for the soul of the Traveler. Climbing onto a jagged ledge just above Bisbee, Spit-Yak whispered in his ear.

"You were a water-bearer in Harness, weren't you? That was a very important position given to a very important man. Do you remember how people looked at you? It was like you were a god."

Bisbee missed how important the people of Harness made him feel. He missed the way his friends and family had looked at him. He knew Charis would hold none of that.

"You're a good man Bisbee, better than most. Return to Harness, and I will make you an elephant rider. They can't attack you when you're on their backs. You will have full control of their power. I will give you true freedom."

Bisbee had never thought of riding the Beasts. If the elephants could not be killed, why not take advantage of them? Why not use their power to rebuild what they destroyed?

"But how can this be done?"

Spit-Yak crawled down from the rocky ledge and sat close to Bisbee, as if he were an old friend. Together they stared into the fire.

"Wordsss, my friend. Powerful wordsss. There are certain phrases that grab the attention of the Beasts and force them to yield their power. You could ask the Eldersss; they know all about riding the elephants."

"What are you talking about?"

"Oh, you didn't know, did you? The Beasts don't need Riders to cause suffering, but there are those from among the Elders of Harness who have chosen to..., shall we say, take advantage of their strength? They use the elephants to maintain a level of fear in Harness. It's how they stay in power. Why do you think Macafee wanted you gone? Bisbee, you were on the verge of exposing him. Your friend Mitch knew all about Macafee. One of the Elders told him."

The Traveler became light-headed. Mitch had known and was trying to warn him... but which Elder had broken ranks? The Leaders of Harness had formed an allegiance with the Beasts, and Spit Yak was at the heart of it. It all began to fit so perfectly.

Bisbee was seized with a new and disturbing fear. Have they taken Avonlea and Lorelai captive? He should be back in Harness, protecting his loved ones. Stephen was fighting in Shedar but was that any better than riding the Beast? The Elders will certainly come to Charis to seek revenge. Bisbee envisioned hoards of Beasts riding over Crossing Bridge into the Land of Charis. Was Marnin strong enough to keep them out?

Bisbee continued to stare into the hot coals, sickened by the possibility of disaster. Chaos was never supposed to be a part of Charis. In the midst of his internal struggle against the lies of Spit Yak, a spark from the fire flew into the air and landed on the writings. Horrified, Bisbee watched as a small flame jumped from the parchment. After blowing it out, his eyes fell on a charred passage in the writings.

"Marnin is the center of all things. He is the magnificence of the morning and the joy of every waiting heart. There is no life without him; there is no victory apart from him; there is no power that can overcome those who trust in him."

Bisbee held the writings close to his chest and breathed a sigh of relief. As he turned away from the demon, he saw movement at the mouth of the cave.

A Black Elephant, standing at the entrance, trumpeted a blast that shook the entire cavern. Bisbee fell forward, landing close to the fire. Writhing in pain, he looked down to see his injured ankle wedged between two rocks. Bisbee cried out for his Master.

Since his fall down Ascending Hill, Bisbee had been plagued by this injury. Staring at his swollen ankle, he became angry with Marnin. Why had the Master not healed it? The puffy ankle seemed to serve no purpose in his journey; yet, the injury persistently dogged his every move. Did the Master not care? As anger turned to a smoldering frustration, Bisbee found himself feeling deep guilt.

Spit-Yak sensed that Bisbee's anger was really directed at Marnin, and it seized the moment.

The demon slowly extended its left hand in an attempt to draw Bisbee's eyes to the dagger it held.

"I've been sent here to offer you freedom from your misery. Abandon your journey, my friend. Who has joined you in your empty pursuit toward a useless hole in the ground? Your own son called you a coward. You have failed to follow the Great Liar. You promised him that you would never leave Charis, and where are you now? In a cave, cowering in fear and despair. Go on, plunge it into your rotten heart and be done with it. The one who sent me beckons you. The glorious one desires your company."

Filled with misery, Bisbee could only stare back at Spit-Yak. Submerged of self-pity, the Traveler looked down at the dagger and saw his reflection. He had no energy to object to Spit-Yak's plan. His association with the Beast was bad enough, but seeing its full implication brought the Traveler so low, he saw no way out. Marnin had mentioned death in the Land; perhaps Bisbee would give it to him.

Staring at the ceiling of his tomb, he wondered if the Master even cared. Did Marnin know what he was going through or even where he was? Sensing Bisbee's pain, Spit-Yak went in for the kill.

"You're worthless Bisbee, a sorry excuse for a man. Your self-loathing is justified: you have caused all of your own misery. Who knows, maybe through your death, Charis will be saved. You are a pathetic failure, a man who in the end finds himself alone. Even your Precious One isn't here to help you."

Spit Yak was telling the truth about one thing. Everything Bisbee had ever done was for himself. His world had always revolved around his own needs, and he was finally seeing it for the first time. He had dismissed anyone and anything standing in the way of his desires. Was his journey to Charis not for his deliverance, his victory and his freedom? Was Marnin nothing more to him than a means to an end? Was the Master nothing more than a useful tool to him? The Traveler found it impossible to refute the creature.

Spit Yak became excited at the suffering of his prey.

Bisbee looked at the demon with empty eyes.

"Do it for me."

"Why should I have the pleasure of killing you? You caused the pain; it's only right that you end it. Here, take the blade: you know where your filthy heart beats."

Reaching out, Bisbee took the dagger from Spit-Yak's hand. Trembling, he stared into the darkness. His life had been a constant battlefield, filled with those wounded by his own hand, and littered with wasted opportunities. The world would be a better place without him. Marnin would have one less problem-child.

Seeing that his work was done, Spit-Yak crawled out of the cave and into the night. Mounting the Black Beast, the creature howled once more at the moon. Spit-Yak had known from the start that he could never lay a hand on one of Marnin's followers. His plan was to discourage Bisbee so that he would take his own life. Leaving the cave, Spit-Yak never anticipated what would happen next.

Buried in the darkness of the cave, the follower of Marnin made his decision. Still holding the cold blade in his hand, Bisbee felt a shame deeper than the moment that he faced the Beast in the field. He was so sick of himself, so sick of it all. In fact, he was sick enough to go to his own funeral and that is exactly what he did. Bisbee ended it all that night...

but not with the blade of Spit-Yak.

Hearing the clanking of metal, the Traveler looked down to see the dagger he had just dropped, dancing on the cave floor.

Broken beyond repair, Bisbee passed through the vortex of his own unworthiness, abandoning himself into Marnin's embrace. Having found no goodness in himself, he forever buried any hope of producing it. Bisbee reached out to a love that he could never merit, choosing to recline in a forgiveness that he could never exhaust. From that day forward, he would expect nothing from himself and find everything in his Master.

Next to the fallen knife lay the writings of Marnin. The morning sun was breaking into the cave, and it gave light to the page before him. Slowly he read.

"You will never be good enough to merit my love and never bad enough to drive me away. I expect nothing from you but an open heart to believe that I have set my favor on you. Simply come to me and all things are yours. You are mine because I have chosen you. The love that I have embraced you with is a love that looks beyond your faults."

The Traveler sat peacefully by the smoldering fire. As his thoughts drifted toward the sunrise of a new day, he realized that he had changed. His heart still cried out for freedom but no longer for selfish gain. He was beginning to understand what it meant to be ready from Marnin's perspective. He had to embrace death in order to obtain life. The Master had been waiting for Bisbee's total abandonment.

Hidden deep beneath the forest floor, in the darkness of the limestone cave, it had all become clear to Bisbee. As a result, a deep rest was beginning to invade the Traveler's soul. He realized he was one step closer to the Well of Chayah.

When Adam chose to reject God, he plunged the entire human race into a condition of sin. The Creator's original design was marred by Adam's move toward independence. As a result, boiling deep within the heart of man is a caldron so polluted that it would be devastating to know its true horror.

Our entire lives, we are encouraged to think for ourselves and to find our own way. To do less would seem robotic and a violation of our freedom to choose our own path. We view the "right to ourselves" as our greatest asset.

The prophet Isaiah gave us a pure definition of sin when he wrote, "All we, like sheep, have gone astray, we have turned everyone to his own way."[1] We may be sheep, but we resist the idea of someone telling us what pasture to graze in or from which stream to drink. The core of Adam's rebellion was his bold assertion that he had a "right to himself." Independence is a manifestation of pure pride. Rejecting the centrality of his Creator, Adam placed himself on the throne of his life. According to Isaiah, sin is "going" our own way; it is "doing" our own thing.

We naturally declare independence from anything that contradicts our view of reality or dares to defy our own logic. We celebrate independence and applaud those who stand on their own two feet, but then we find that God has condemned the very thing we applaud. It is obvious that we need God's perspective on the matter to form the correct reality.

At this point it would be good to go back in time and revisit our ancestors, Adam and Eve. The conditions and environment that predated sin's disastrous arrival will reveal a God that had a much different design for man than we ever imagined. Seen from the Creator's viewpoint, the horrifying effect of sin will be evident.

As we peer through the foliage, keep in mind that the fall of Adam and Eve into sin was our fall as well. When Adam and Eve bit the forbidden fruit, we chewed it with them. The apple never falls far from the tree, so even though the event took place long ago, it is relevant to our present-day situation.

Within the triune community of the Godhead, the creation of man was not born out of need. "Need" is a creature-word, absent within the One who is self-existent.[2] The issue of need has always been, and will always be, on the side of humanity. God, being all-sufficient, has need of nothing. Adam "needed" his Creator for life, while God "desired" intimacy with His created one. God is glorified in Himself; man is not needed in the equation. By mankind's freedom to honor God's self-evidence, He is indeed glorified.

With His spoken word, God fashioned a world of perpetual delight with the creation of man in view.[3] After hand-crafting a body for Adam, capable of experiencing the world He had designed, He placed the first man in a garden, described as paradise.[4] Before Adam drew his first breath, his Creator anticipated his needs.

Since God did not "need" mankind, the decision to breathe life into Adam was born on the wings of pure love found within Himself in an overflow to Adam. In designing the world, God's ability to call something out of nothing was an expression of His power; however, when He formed man, love was the motivating factor. God's intense passion in the creation of man found its origin in the heart of the Father, the Son and the Holy Spirit. A deep desire for intimate fellowship and communion was the Creator's heartbeat for His image bearer. God shared intimate fellowship with His created son as they walked together in the cool of the day. The joy that Adam experienced during those afternoon walks is beyond our ability to comprehend.

To further bless the first man, God fashioned for him a woman.[5] She would be his companion, to share in all the beauty and joy that he was experiencing. As Adam embraced his bride, a greater scene could not be imagined. The Triune God surrounded the first couple with infinite love and care. Their purpose was fully revealed in the garden: Adam and Eve were created for an intimate connection with their Creator. They were designed to draw life from the One who loved them supremely and desired their greatest good.

Then a terrible choice was made which still affects us all.[6] Adam and Eve willfully chose to go their own way. They turned their backs on the One who had given them everything. The result is the tragic history of the struggle of mankind through the centuries to find peace and fulfillment.

We are so far removed from the scene of the crime that we fail to see the horror of the event. An independent spirit was instantly infused into the first couple as they scrambled to cover their nakedness.[7] Down through the corridors of time, humanity now applauds and rewards independence as if it were the apex of our existence. In an expression of full-blown rebellion, we go our own way, distancing ourselves from God. Shockingly, the "right to ourselves," is humanity's greatest sin.

A greater paradigm shift cannot be imagined. Everything changed for all mankind that day in the garden. Life became centered on self. Building kingdoms for the glory of men became the new "normal," and a deep sense of loneliness pervaded humanity.

If God, in His mercy, did not shed light into the deep recesses of our heart and show us our sinfulness, then we would spend our life mining about in Plato's cave of darkness. The enemy finds his greatest advantage when we are ignorant of the depth of sin within us.

The method that God uses to bring us to this moment of discovery is simple and direct. He stands idly by and allows us to fall flat on our faces. Through circumstances and people, He constantly reveals our selfish spirits.

Brought to our lowest point, we finally see what the Lord has known all along. Apart from Him we have no life, no desire to love Him, and absolutely no ability to conquer sin. The more we understand and experience God's grace, the more aware we are of our sinfulness.

Evan Hopkins once wrote, "To learn sin's true nature we must look at it, not only in relation to ourselves, but in relation to God; we must regard it in connection with His infinite justice, and holiness and love. It is only in that light that we shall understand its real character."[8]

God's goal in revealing this truth about our flesh is to lead us to an end of ourselves.[9] Allowing us to fail is His prescribed method. Natural energies have to die out before grace is extended. Peter was confident in his ability to be loyal to Jesus, but he did not know grace until he denied the Master three times. Moses thought killing an Egyptian equated to the deliverance of his people.[10] It took forty years on the backside of a desert to bring him to a place of complete reliance on the Lord. God is in no hurry; He waits patiently as we trudge through the years of struggle.

We will never abandon self-effort until we reach "rock bottom" and confess our condition. We have fought a losing battle; we have waged a war against a power too great for us. Our flesh cannot be conquered by our efforts. After digging for years, we finally hit hardpan and throw our bent and cracked shovel to the ground.

The deliverance of Jesus Christ is directed toward the soul that has abandoned all hope in human enterprise. Until then, our focus will continue to be on our performance rather than on Christ.

God never leads us into sin, but He certainly uses our failures and struggles to reveal our need for Him.[11] Frustration is a wonderful diving board into the pool of God's grace. At that moment, even a belly flop is enjoyable. When the great spiritual crisis arrives, and we finally give up hope in ourselves, it is a welcomed relief. Instead of being disheartened, we are actually encouraged. Finally, we cry out in full agreement with the Apostle Paul, "In my flesh dwells 'no' good thing."[12]

Walking out of the cave of self-preoccupation into the sunlight of His grace, we are free from the pressure of performance. The need to impress others is gone. No more vigorous attempts to defend ourselves from insult and injury. At this juncture of life when we give up trying, He takes over. And what a glorious "takeover" it is!

This type of teaching flies in the face of the modern approach, which spares the believer of any discomfort. The church today has been stroked and pampered for so long by shallow platitudes that she has little stomach for the truth that bruises and crushes her elephant sized ego.

In light of this fact, I do not hesitate to proclaim the truth concerning the flesh, knowing that it is our only hope. Until we see the elephant in the room and more specifically within our own hearts, we will never cry out in despair, "O wretched man that I am! Who shall deliver me from the body of this death?" Until we come to that moment of despair, we will never join Paul in declaring, "I thank God through Jesus Christ my Lord."[13]

It is a wonderful day when we attend our own funeral and realize that the body lying there can do nothing to please God. At that moment, the only thing that makes good sense is to close the wooden box and walk away. The darkest night yields to a glorious sunrise when the front door of the funeral home swings wide open, and we step out into the light. Weep no tears for the dearly departed: he was nothing but a rascal.

CHAPTER 15

THE WELL OF CHAYAH

The warmth of the morning sun welcomed Bisbee as he emerged from the cave. He was relieved to be rid of Spit-Yak and for that matter, himself. The encounter with the demon helped set him free from the burden of believing that he could conquer his Beast alone. The Traveler had not realized the pressure he had been living under while carrying the heavy burden of self-importance. Bisbee's empty visions of self-grandeur lay smoldering in the cave. The weight of the world had been lifted off of his shoulders.

All that Bisbee had counted as precious was lying in the golden glow of the cave fire. Life and death were now trivial matters in comparison to knowing Marnin. Bisbee had always thought that life was a result of the energies and enterprises of his own making. He now knew that the true value of life was not found within himself. The experience of the previous night had been painful, yet, it was worth it all. Bisbee was enjoying the blessing of having written on his own tombstone.

Shielding his eyes from the sun, he could see the white farmhouse just ahead through a patch of blackberry bushes. A soft breeze filled his lungs with fresh air, which was a welcome relief from what he had breathed in the cave the night before. The branches above him danced in the wind, causing the rain-kissed leaves to shower his matted hair.

As the Red Robin flew gracefully overhead, Bisbee instinctively knew that today was the day he would discover the mystery of the Well of Chayah. He was confident that by sunset his questions would be answered.

The Traveler was amazed at how close to Charis he had been the night before. Spit-Yak must have known that their encounter in the cave would be the last chance to keep Bisbee from the Well. The importance of what he was about to discover had been clear to the demon. Like an animal backed into a corner, Spit-Yak had fought with all the poison flowing through its vile veins. Marnin had not placed Spit-Yak in the cave, but the Master had certainly used the moment to bring Bisbee to an end of himself.

After having crossed over a wet ditch, Bisbee found himself standing between two, large, maple trees. He had finally reached his destination. It felt good to be back in Charis.

The scene before him was just as he had imagined. The old white clapboard farmhouse stood two stories high and was capped with a rusty tin roof. Built in the shape of a large square box, the front of the house was as flat as a pancake. A middle-aged woman hung out of an upstairs window, carefully cleaning the glass from the storm of the previous night. The woman turned toward the Traveler and smiled. Bisbee smiled back but inwardly, feared that she would fall.

In the front yard, two stone sidewalks, cracked and broken by age, led to two separate front doors. Large, black ants busied themselves in the crevices of the walkways, marching back and forth, oblivious to the excitement of the day. A covered porch was attached to the right side of the house, and at the base of the structure was a metal trap door. The front yard was covered with a soft rye grass, which was shaded by the two large maple trees that Bisbee stood between.

A lilac bush grew on the right side of the porch and under it stood Charlie and Beatrice, deep in conversation. He had never been so happy in all of his life to see a muskrat and an owl. There had been moments in the cave that he feared he would never make it out, and when he saw the two of them standing under the lilac he almost shouted for joy.

Bisbee was about to call out to the pair when the owl spotted him. Together they turned toward Bisbee, evaluating his condition. Charlie noticed that Bisbee was relaxed. Beatrice was just happy he had made it out of the forest, and spreading her massive wings, she flew off toward Living Stream. Bisbee was surprised that Beatrice had had a reaction at all.

Bisbee had hoped to see Marnin, but he was not there. The Traveler felt, at times, that Marnin was unpredictable. When Bisbee was sure the Master would be in a certain place at a particular time, he did not appear, and in the most unexpected moments, Bisbee found him standing there. He found it impossible to anticipate the Master's next move, which forced Bisbee to trust that Marnin was watching over him. The Traveler knew Marnin had a reason for everything he did.

"You look different, my friend."

Charlie had walked over to where Bisbee was standing under the maple.

"What do you mean?" asked the Traveler.

"Oh, I don't know, more relaxed, less anxious?"

"A night in a cave will take the wind out of you."

"You're a different man than I met at Crossing Bridge," observed Charlie.

"Yes, I think I am."

"Sit down, Bisbee, I need to tell you something."

The Traveler grew anxious as he sat down at the base of the maple and leaned his back against its smooth bark.

"It was all necessary, every bit of it. Marnin offers no shortcuts to the Well. He is relentless until his followers see the truth concerning their condition. The Master graciously allows his sojourners to choose their own path; however, eventually they all end up in a cave. He knows that those who seek him will never see the mystery of the Well until they have given up on themselves. Skeletons and sadness litter the path to self-abandonment. Marnin is the torchbearer in the black cave, revealing darkness within us that we never knew existed. Pain and difficulty have brought you to your lowest place, Bisbee. He finds no pleasure in your pain, no joy in your suffering. They are simply the tools he uses to bring you to your cave of self-revelation. It is great relief to know the truth."

"I thought I was ready at Crossing Bridge. When I entered Charis, I imagined I could just walk up to the Well of Chayah, and by one look into its depths, understand it all."

Charlie smiled.

"Most of Marnin's followers think that they know all there is to know about the Well. Standing far off, they speak of its importance, knowing little of its mystery. Do you see the porch?"

"Yes." responded Bisbee.

"Once a week, a group meets there to talk about the Well. They examine every conceivable angle, studying the composition of the stone and the type of moss growing at its base. They live in a land of shadows. No true sunlight ever breaks in on them."

"Really. I'd like to meet them."

Charlie smiled again.

"Talking about the Well isn't the same as looking into its depths."

"But I could learn from them." Bisbee protested.

Charlie patiently continued.

"Bisbee, listen to me. One look into the Well of Chayah is worth a thousand explanations from the porch. A crawfish out of the creek tastes better than one out of a book. Besides, they're members of the Tribe of Gibbor. Each week they draw up new battle plans for a fight they can't win, in a war that has long since been won."

The two sat together in a comfortable silence, enjoying a friendship that was free from the nuisance of needless dialog. A large, yellow tomcat limped across the front yard, blood pouring from what was left of his face. A steady stream of blood dripped into the grass as it looked for a place in the bushes to lie down and die.

"Poor cat," Bisbee observed.

"His name is Mister, and he should have known better than to hunt woodchucks. When you boil it all down Bisbee, life is about choices."

The Traveler stood up and looked down at Charlie. The muskrat had been a loyal guide, and Bisbee would forever be grateful that Marnin had sent him. He would never again put limitations on whom the Master could use to show him truth.

"Charlie…"

"I know. Don't say it. Once a muskrat starts to cry there's no stopping. Besides, I have an image to uphold. What if the possum strolled by and saw me blubbering like an idiot?"

Bisbee smiled and shook his head.

"Go my friend, the mystery awaits you. You will not be disappointed."

A nervous flock of sparrows landed in the nearby apple tree, anticipating Bisbee's walk toward the Well. Passing by the porch, he entered the shade of the lilac. Bisbee pushed aside the lower branches of the huge bush and entered a small, cleared-out area that had been hidden from view. Covered with moss and sitting on a small stony ledge was the Well of Chayah. An old, wooden bucket with a long thick rope hung on a hook next to the Well. A large, brown toad sat on the top of the well, studying the Traveler.

Bisbee was immediately struck with how ordinary it all seemed. Nothing attracted him to the Well; nothing captivated him about the setting. He had expected something more impressive. Bisbee had imagined that seeing the Well would overwhelm him with a deep sense of reverence, but instead, the taste of *vanilla was in his mouth. The toad was a fitting guardian to such an ordinary scene. The moment was neither exciting nor surreal.*

Bisbee looked down at the toad. The ugly croaker sat like royalty and peered at the Traveler with condescending eyes. Deciding to take a closer look, Bisbee stepped forward. As he came within a few steps of the Well, the toad rose up on his hind feet and spoke with a deep voice.

"Not what you expected? Did you think your experience in the cave was enough? The shadow of the Beast that hangs over you is more than you understand."

The wart-covered amphibian had little patience for spectators at the Well, and so he got straight to the point.

"Charlie was wrong. You're not ready. Go away."

Turning to leave, the toad paused and looked back toward Bisbee.

"Come back when you're free of your childish expectations. Go fight in the Forest of Shedar like the others who just stand and stare at the Well. On second thought, don't return."

Bisbee was stunned. Even a toad could see through his misgivings and disillusionment.

"You're wrong...ah,ah."

"The name is Wilbur and I am never wrong."

"Well, today you are... Wilbur," insisted Bisbee.

"Go ahead, look in. You'll see for yourself."

Bisbee placed his hands on the rock wall and looked into the black hole. As his eyes adjusted to the darkness, he saw nothing but a rusty, toy rifle wedged between two rocks. Too deep to retrieve, but shallow enough to see, it had been thrown in years ago.

Bisbee stared into the lilac bush. The disappointment he felt was more than he could bear. He had traveled so far and been through so much. The toad had been right, just as he said he was. He looked up to see if Wilbur was enjoying his humiliation, but instead, the guardian of the Well had bowed his head. Bisbee turned and saw Marnin.

Without saying a word, the Master stepped forward and placed his hand on Bisbee's shoulder. Turning him back toward the Well, Marnin spoke gently in the Traveler's ear.

"Wilbur was right, you're not ready Bisbee."

The Traveler's heart sunk in his chest. Marnin had spoken it with his own lips, and now Bisbee knew it was true. Tears welled up in his eyes as his body began to shake with emotion. Collapsing to the ground, he felt the strong hands of Marnin picking him back up and setting him on his feet.

"Wait, I'm not done. Wilbur spoke the truth, but you need to understand that no one is ever ready to see what I'm going to show you. You cannot understand what happened in the Well apart from me."

Together Bisbee and his Master leaned over the Well and looked into the bottomless abyss. With eyes that were now fully open, he saw Marnin falling in the Well. Bisbee grabbed the stonewall to keep from slipping. Looking again, he saw a second man falling with Marnin further and further in the darkness until they were both gone. Who was the man with Marnin in the Well? Did he really want to know? Terrified, Bisbee looked up at the Master.

"It was you, Bisbee. The man next to me was you."

Stunned, he backed away, unable to feel the lilac branches digging into his back. Was he dead? If he had died, then Marnin must be dead also, but how could these things be? The Master stepped over to Bisbee and gently took him by the arm. Without a word, they returned to the Well.

"Look again, my friend."

The Traveler would never be able to explain what he saw next, but the knowledge of it would change his life forever. Forcing himself to look back into the Well, he saw those same two men rising out of the blackness. Bisbee watched with great astonishment, as both he and Marnin returned out of the dark pit and into the glorious sunlight. The shadow of the Beast faded into the distance and even though Bisbee could still see it, his separation from it welded deeply into his heart. The Master had brought him back from the dead, and Bisbee was alive in a way that he had never known before. Overwhelmed, all Bisbee could do was stare at Marnin.

"What happened in the Well is the key to it all, Bisbee. When I fell, long ago, I took you with me, and in doing so, I separated you from the Beast. Its power over you was broken in the Well of Chayah. You have been living in fear and defeat because you were unaware that the Beast's reign of terror was finished. This victory is not something you gain by fighting the Beasts. It is a gift that I have already given you because of our fall together in the Well. Now that you know the truth, it is important that you respond to it."

Bisbee looked up at Marnin.

"How do I respond to what I have just seen?"

"Rest, Bisbee, simply rest in what I have done."

As a result of what happened in the Well of Chayah, Bisbee now knew that complete victory over the Beast belonged to the Master. He could enter into that victory, but the triumph would always be connected to Marnin.

Bisbee now understood why it was important to be ready for this moment. Pride had to be stripped from his heart in order for him to receive the gift. No sense of achievement attached itself to what happened in the Well. No credit to the follower of Marnin could be granted for a victory he had no part in winning. Astonished by the simplicity and power of the Well of Chayah, Bisbee stood in reverent silence, gazing at the Master.

"You don't have to say anything, Bisbee. I loved you long before I met you at Sanford Ledge. There is more depth in the Well than you will ever understand."

Stepping forward, Bisbee fell into the arms of Marnin. He had discovered the mystery of the Well of Chayah at last. The man who thought he had to prove his worth to Marnin was now buried. Rising to a new dawn was a heart chasing after the one who had been chasing after him. The years that he had spent wandering the countryside of Harness were over. Bisbee's fall into the Well was the death that Marnin had spoken of, and as a result, the endless battle to defeat the Beast was in the past. His rise up out of the Well with Marnin was the source of life found in Charis.

True to the letters that Mitch had given him, the Well of Chayah was a place of death and a source of life. Bisbee looked up into the limitless blue sky, as tears ran down his cheeks. The Traveler was home.

Who is Jesus Christ? What did He accomplish on the Cross? Real Christian living does not begin until the answers to these two questions are fully understood and personally integrated into the life of the follower of Christ.

Jesus Christ was God in the flesh, making His Cross the Cross of God.[1] His death made the redemption of humanity available. The debt of sin that all men owe was buried with Christ.[2] He took mankind with Him into the tomb. Every human being was plunged into the dark abyss of the grave.

In ancient Israel, God established a system of sacrifice for the sins of the people. Blood flowed like water from the courts of the Temple in Jerusalem on the Day of Atonement. The blade of the priests slit the neck of lamb after lamb. Year after year, this offering of blood only covered the sins of Israel. Beyond covering "sins," Christ dealt, once for all, with sin itself.[3] Jesus, being the "Lamb of God," took away the sin of the world. As a result, God does not hold man responsible for the sin of Adam.[4]

Jesus Christ has fully paid the price for sin, and in doing so, He has taken responsibility for original sin. This is why Paul can confidently declare that God has reconciled all things to Himself. When Adam and Eve rebelled, they were barred from the Garden of Eden. When Adam sinned, he turned his back on God. Through the sacrifice of Christ, God has removed the barrier of sin and has turned back toward Adam. Because of the work of Christ, God welcomes the penitent sinner home with open arms.

This does not mean that all men are saved. He holds men responsible for their decision to believe on Christ. Only those who respond by faith in His redemptive work are redeemed.[5] Those who have believed on Christ have obeyed the gospel (which is the death, burial, and resurrection of Jesus). These "redeemed ones" are then resurrected out of their spiritual deadness toward God, having received new life. The same Spirit that raised Jesus from the dead now lives in those who have believed on Christ.[6]

As believers, we embrace the truth that Christ died for us. We rejoice in the doctrine of vicarious atonement, which is the truth that Christ died in our place.[7] He took the wrath of God that we deserved, so that we could be forgiven and restored. The first great reality of the gospel is that the penalty for our sins has been forgiven.

The second great reality of the gospel is that when Jesus died, we died with Him.[8] In our co-crucifixion with Christ, God separated us from sin. Our victory over the flesh was purchased at the moment Jesus cried out, "It is finished!" The mystery of what happened there is the fountainhead of all blessing to the disciple of Christ.

While enjoying life, we rarely think of death, but it will certainly come. When we die, our bodies are separated from our spirit, and our spirit returns to God. Death is the "Great Separator." The warning God gave to Adam and Eve was that in the day they disobeyed Him, they would surely die. In that day they did die in their relationship with God. They were separated spiritually from their Creator.

When we died with Christ, He separated us from sin. Sin still dwells in us, but we are dead in relation to it.[9] He did not remove our carnality when He saved us; He separated us from it by our co-crucifixion with Christ. The flesh is very much alive, but we are dead to it. Our victory over sin is brought to bear when we understand that we are separated from it. As a result, it has no power over us.[10]

If men choose not to believe in the gospel, they remain buried in spiritual darkness, and their eternal damnation looms over them. They are in danger of spending eternity in hell because they have rejected Christ and His redemptive work on the cross.[11] The sacrifice of the Cross has no effect on the unrepentant sinner.

The truth of the believers' death with Christ is a fact to be accepted, not a moment to be experienced. We do not cause our death to sin; it is an established fact. We do not need to concentrate on any particular sin in our lives and then pray to die a "deeper death" to that sin. We are already dead to it. Our crucifixion with Christ is as much a fact as the historical Cross of Jesus. We will receive no victory over sin until we know and rest in the fact that our death with Christ is a finished reality.[12]

You may argue from your own experience, "I feel very much alive to sin." There is no more common experience than the battle against our own self-destructive behavior. The raging forces within us all, seek to undermine what we know to be right and pure. The fury of sin rushes over us like a tsunami wave. None of us denies the presence of sin that desires to take us captive. This is why the Bible says that we are to walk by faith and not by sight.[13] Our whole being tells us that we are alive to the flesh, but the Scriptures declare that we are dead to sin. Faith must always come from revealed truth that we find in the Bible. The just shall live by faith.

The history of Adam and the terrible choice he made to rebel against God is the history of all mankind. You may object and argue that you were not there when Adam sinned but actually, you were. You and I were in the loins of Adam when he decided to plunge us all into sin. By our natural birth we all carry the likeness of the first Adam. The second Adam, being Christ, came to redeem the first Adam (humanity), by His death on the Cross.

In considering mankind, God only recognizes these two men, the first Adam and the second Adam. The first Adam was the first created man, and the second Adam is Christ. Under these two federal heads, God deals with all of humanity.

When a man yields to Christ, he is reborn into a new likeness. God takes the man who has believed on Christ out of the first Adam and places him in Christ, (the second Adam).[14] In the same way that we inherited the history of Adam by our first birth, we now possess the history of Christ by virtue of our rebirth. Our history in the first Adam began when he sinned in the Garden of Eden and our history in Christ began after He cried, "It is finished!" At that point we, as believers, entered into death with Him. When He rose from the dead, we were raised to newness of life. Concerning the power of sin in our lives, our co-crucifixion with Christ means that we have been separated from sin, and its power has been broken.[15]

Listen carefully. By the sovereign act of the Almighty God, those who have come to Christ, have been placed in Christ. Based solely on this fact, we have died to sin and been made alive unto God. We did nothing to cause this, and we can do nothing to change it. It is true whether we believe it or not. When we rest in this reality, we begin to draw the benefits of our position: namely, victory over sin.[16]

Death ends all conflict. If I am dead to something, it has no power over me. Imagine working for a difficult boss, and nothing you ever do pleases him. Life in the shop was a daily struggle. Finally, there comes the day of your retirement and after saying your goodbyes and accepting your "gold watch," you drive home. Checking your phone messages, you discover a voicemail from your old boss demanding you come into work early the next day. How would you respond to the message? Would you set your alarm and wake up early the next day? No! Of course you wouldn't! Your old boss has no power over you; you are retired. Your separation from the workplace means he has lost all authority over you.

Sin is no longer your master. You are no longer in bondage to the power of the flesh because you are dead in relation to it. It is a reality to be received by faith because Christ has finished the work of redemption. The Cross of Christ is God's only answer to the power of sin in our lives. The gospel is the power of God unto salvation for everyone who believes.[17]

The gospel fully redeems us from sin. The blood of Jesus releases us from the penalty of sin, while the Cross delivers us from the power of sin. The presence of sin will be removed once we leave this world and receive our new bodies. Praise the Lord! His redemption is eternal, and it is a finished work. May you rest in His victory!

CHAPTER 16

WOODEN SPEARS

Bisbee spent the next few hours asking Marnin a thousand questions. What he had seen in the Well opened his eyes. It was the "peace" of the puzzle that Bisbee had been missing. He now rested in a new reality that dominated his thinking and encouraged his heart. The years of slowly starving in Harness had created an emptiness that Charis was now filling.

Walking down Ascending Hill, he remembered the eagle soaring in the wind and the never-ending flow of Living Stream. Reality wrapped in mystery was now possible. After struggling with the concept of death, he was now able to reconcile that it was his death, which led to life. The hunger for truth he experienced in those early days with Marnin had returned.

"Bisbee, you've heard enough for one day. Let's pick this back up when both of us are not so distracted with the joy of discovery."

Marnin smiled and turned to walk away.

"You, distracted?"

"No, I was being kind. I really do have to go. My seat on Broken Dam is calling my name."

Bisbee was intrigued.

"Why do you spend so much time at Broken Dam?"

"It was the place where I renewed the valley. That was a great day. I love releasing life, Bisbee."

And with that, the Master turned and walked away.

Bisbee had no difficulty bidding Marnin adieu, for he now possessed a deeper awareness of their union. Sitting back down by the Well, the Victor rested his eyes.

Charlie had been right as usual. One look into the Well of Chayah had given Bisbee an understanding of his Beast and Marnin's victory over it. The energies of the day had left Bisbee washed in a peaceful exhaustion. He could finally rest. As he stared into the flickering leaves of the lilac bush, the Victor fell fast asleep.

Hearing the shuffling of leaves, Bisbee cracked open one eye and saw Charlie speaking with Wilbur under the porch overhang. Closing his eyes, he sat still against the Well, intent upon listening to their conversation.

"It appears as though we have a lazy one here," Wilbur huffed.

Charlie grinned.

"He's wandered so long; it's good to see him settled."

The bumpy toad hopped over next to Bisbee and peered curiously into his closed eyelids. A small fly landed on Bisbee's shoe and was quickly snatched up by the toad's sticky tongue.

"It's always a beautiful moment when travelers finally see what Marnin's done," said Wilbur.

Charlie agreed.

"I never tire of it. The Well is the last place they look for answers, and the struggling stops when they find it."

Charlie walked over and joined Wilbur. Looking into the Victor's face, the muskrat smiled again.

"Bisbee is special to me."

The toad frowned and shook his fat head.

"You say that about every traveler."

"No, this one is different. I liked him from the start."

Struggling to keep his eyes closed, Bisbee fought back a smile. He thought back to when he first met Charlie at Crossing Bridge. He had been wary of a talking muskrat, but Charlie had won his confidence and more importantly, his friendship. Bisbee could not wait to introduce him to Avonlea.

"Have you told him about his ankle?" asked the toad.

"No, he'll find out soon enough."

Bisbee resisted the temptation to open his eyes and ask about his injury. He was learning to be patient about such things.

"Are the others on their way?"

"Beatrice flew up to Ascending Hill to see if she could spot them," Charlie answered.

Tears filled Bisbee's closed eyelids, forcing their way through the pressed skin and down the sides of his face. Was Avonlea close to entering Charis? What about the others? Anxiety growing within him, Bisbee willed himself to remain still against the mossy stone.

The sun streamed through the lilac, warming the Victor's face. A gentle breeze blew against his chest calming his spirit. He wished he could bathe in this moment forever, but he knew his journey had only now begun. Wilbur and Charlie chatted on about the different travelers they had helped. Occasionally they would break into an argument concerning minute details that made no difference to the eventual outcome of the story. The friendly banter continued until Bisbee, at last, fell back asleep.

Awakening to the song of the sparrows in the apple tree, Bisbee wondered where his friends had gone. The sun, which had not yet fully risen, cast sleepy shadows on the stone steps leading down to the apple tree. Climbing to his feet, he brushed the lilac leaves off his pants and headed down the path to find Charlie. Reaching the bottom of the trail, he rounded the bend and saw his friend sitting at the base of the tree, enjoying its shade and eating its fruit.

"Finally woke up, I see."

"You and that toad are quite a pair," remarked Bisbee.

"He's a good enough sort. He just can't get his stories straight."

Leaning against the tree trunk, Bisbee plucked an apple. He bit deeply into the fruit and looked toward Ascending Hill.

"I haven't slept that peacefully in months, maybe years."

Charlie looked up at Bisbee.

"Real sleep starts with the soul being at rest. Fear robs many a night."

Bisbee looked in the direction of the cornfields. Broken stalks, trampled by the Beast, stood crooked in the field.

"I need to go find it, don't I?"

Charlie shook his head.

"No need of that, it will find you soon enough."

Bisbee did not have long to wait. Like a train pulling into a station, the moment of truth arrived. The roar of an elephant from within the barn shook the ground, causing the sparrows to take flight. Charlie watched for Bisbee's reaction *with great interest. The first of many defining moments was about to be thrust into the Victor's lap.*

Bisbee stepped from under the apple tree out into the open yard. Without hesitation, the Victor walked until he reached the center of the lawn and then, as if bracing himself for the battle ahead, spread his feet wide apart.

The Beast roared again, causing Bisbee to clutch his ears in pain. A thunderous explosion shook the old structure as the Beast crashed through the barn wall, landing only feet from Bisbee. The Victor shielded himself as the broken boards landed like spears all around him. The furious creature reared back on its hind feet and trumpeted another deafening blast. The hot discharge of its heavy breath blew Bisbee's hair back, leaving him nauseated.

Tempted to retreat into fear, the Victor stepped backwards. As the Beast towered over him, Bisbee felt as weak as a lamb before a lion. The Well of Chayah had given him confidence that when this moment came, he would be victorious; but, instead he found himself afraid and in a state of panic.

Bisbee took another step backward and when he did, the unseen hand of the Master played a trump card that the Victor had not anticipated. An intense bolt of pain from his injured ankle shot straight through him, traveling razor fast, until it reached his brain. Losing his balance, he fell into the grass, clutching his swollen foot. The Beast closed in for the kill but when it did, Bisbee looked back at the Well. Recalling his death with Marnin and their rise together into the sunlight, Bisbee uttered the one word that changed everything.

"Rest."

Standing to his feet he faced his greatest enemy. The fury of the elephant was greater than he had ever known, and yet in that moment Bisbee knew he possessed the upper hand. The Well was enough. Bisbee had died to the Beast, and its power over him was broken. Its reign of terror was finally finished.

The Beast stepped backward, fear filling its once furious eyes. Turning a sickly pale, the once intimidating creature appeared as harmless as a field mouse. Bisbee stood in amazement as it backed away toward the barn. Finally, he had tasted real victory. His heart filled with gratitude, Bisbee turned back toward Charlie, but his friend had vanished.

Looking back at the Beast, cowering amidst the broken timbers, Bisbee was amazed at the simplicity of it all. His wounded ankle had reminded him of his need to look away from himself and to the Well. Bisbee now understood that his fall down Ascending Hill had been a gift from Marnin. The weakness of his ankle would be a constant reminder that his strength was in the Master. By keeping his eyes fixed on the Well and away from himself, Bisbee would never have to fear the Beast again. The wound that he had dragged through Charis had turned out to be a friend rather than an enemy.

CHAPTER 17

THE WILLOW TREE

The morning sun rose in its full glory over the old barn, exposing a deep wound in the head of the Beast. Was the injury a result of their encounter, or had it always been there? The wound was crusted over with dried blood, but when Bisbee looked a second time he saw a fresh tear. Perhaps a shattered plank from the barn had found its mark.

Noticing Bisbee staring at its open wound, the creature quickly turned away and retreated back into the darkness of the old barn. The Victor knew that he had not seen the last of the Beast.

Bisbee turned and headed back in the direction of the farmhouse. Passing under the tree, he plucked an apple and walked up the stone path to the Well. Wilbur was gone, and Charlie was nowhere to be found. All that could be heard was the rustling of maple leaves from a stout west wind.

Polishing the apple on his sleeve, Bisbee looked at his skewed reflection. He was a changed man and grateful for it. After a time of rest in the shade of the lilac, Bisbee climbed the steps of the porch that overlooked the Land of Charis. As he walked to the end of the porch, the valley came into full view. Bisbee thought about his experiences in this land and all that he had learned since his arrival.

The gentle slopes of Ascending Hill, with its soft green clover, lay before him. The memory of Horatio C. Goldspinner made him smile. Looking to the top of the hill, he saw red smoke rising in the Wood. The people of Glassy Pond were apparently busy with their daily rituals. As his eyes scanned Living Stream, he spotted Hugabone setting a trap in the tall grass. Behind him lay the thick Forest of Shedar and the dark Cave of Spit-Yak.

The journey had been wild and dangerous, but the guiding hand of Marnin could now be seen at every turn. The final destination of the Well of Chayah had been worth every hardship, along with every moment of confusion and discouragement. He now saw that every challenge had prepared him for the Well. The bitter taste of Harness was gone, having been replaced with the sweetness of Charis.

Hearing a sound, he turned to see Charlie sitting on the rail of the porch, chewing on a stalk of hay.

He was glad to see his old friend again.

"You know, you haven't seen the last of the Beast," stated Charlie.

"I know."

"Good."

Charlie pulled a fresh stalk of hay from his back pocket.

"You did well out there."

"You mean Marnin did well." Bisbee responded.

"Touché, my friend."

After exchanging a smile, Charlie continued.

"Bisbee, turn around. I want to show you something."

The Victor turned back toward the valley, and when he did, he saw it filled with the followers of Marnin. Going about their duties with a light heart, they appeared carefree. Women were working in the field, as men labored to clean what they had killed in the forest. Bisbee noticed that a few of them were directing the others, but the atmosphere was so different than that of Harness. Bisbee wondered if these people of Charis struggled with anything.

"It's not that they don't have struggles, Bisbee. It's that they've learned how to leave them with Marnin."

Bisbee had forgotten that Charlie could read his mind.

"They seem so relaxed. How do they get anything done?"

Charlie frowned. "It's not about what they accomplish, Bisbee; it's about the love they have for the Master and thus, each other. In Charis you are not alone. You are now joined to a company of those who leave their struggles with the Master. Their sole purpose is to enjoy Marnin and nothing more."

Bisbee was glad to know he had new friends. The thought of sharing what he had discovered with others who understood Charis was encouraging. He only wished that Avonlea had been one of the women in the field. As Bisbee glanced toward Ascending Hill, loneliness gnawed in the pit of his stomach.

With the thunderous flapping of wings, Beatrice excitedly announced her arrival at the porch. Out of breath, she turned to the Victor.

"Do you see them?"

"See who?"

Beatrice shook her head.

"Look toward Ascending Hill."

Cupping his hand over his eyes, Bisbee fell silent.

"You humans are as blind as bats. Come with me, I'll show you."

Lifting her massive wings, she paused and turned back toward Bisbee. Exerting no effort to hide her frustration, the barn owl stared at the Victor.

"Oh, I forgot. You can't fly either."

Beatrice lifted herself up and grabbed Bisbee's shirt with her claws. Together they made their way down the path that led to Crossing Bridge. Traveling at a rapid pace, they rounded the barn and started down the road beyond the old machine shed. Passing the walnut tree, Bisbee hardly noticed the crunching sound of crushed shells under his feet.

Pausing in the trail to wipe the tears from his eyes, Bisbee looked up toward the crest of Ascending Hill. The scene before him was beyond anything he could have hoped for or imagined. A large group of travelers was descending Ascending Hill and leading the way was his old friend Mitch. Bisbee quickly scanned the crowd for Avonlea, but he could not find her in the group. His breaths became shorter and shorter until he thought he would suffocate. He could not have possibly gone through so much to lose the love of his life? Marnin had made no promises in this regard. And then, as he approached Crossing Bridge, he heard a voice.

"Bisbee, I'm over here."

The voice came from under the willow, but the leaf filled branches hung so low that Bisbee saw nothing but greenery. Suddenly, a strong, west wind blew down Ascending Hill, lifting several branches into the air, and there stood Avonlea. She was poised on the same rock he had rested on only a few days before. As a tear rolled down his cheek, his tall frame grew as weak as a stretched rubber band. Their locked eyes penned endless, unwritten volumes of the love they shared.

"I came ahead of the others. I had to see you. Bisbee, is the land all we've hoped for?"

"It's grander than you can know."

Walking across the Bridge, Bisbee embraced his bride. Her soft touch instantly healed the months of loneliness he had endured without her. Burying his face in her long hair, Bisbee breathed in deeply. Her scent comforted him. Looking over Avonlea's shoulder, Bisbee spotted Mitch.

"Save one of those for me, old friend."

Mitch was walking toward Bisbee with a wide grin. Happy to see that his friend had fully recovered from his heart attack, they shared a hug tighter than two bears after months of hibernation.

"Bisbee, I want you to meet someone."

Bisbee looked curiously into Mitch's eyes. Stepping up next to the trio was one of the Elders of Harness. Bisbee moved backward, uncertain of the possible intentions of a man he was not sure he could trust. Bisbee had been set free from the bondage of Harness, but the sight of Tourgen caused his spirit to recoil.

Tourgen reached his hand out to Bisbee, hoping for a return gesture. None came. Confused, Bisbee stood frozen in the moment. Mitch finally spoke.

"Bisbee, you thought the green letters that you received were from an old friend, but they were from Tourgen. He discovered this land of Charis long before any of us."

Bisbee was bewildered. Why did this Elder of Harness feel the need to conceal his true identity? Even as the thought swirled in his mind, he answered his own question. Bisbee knew he would have never trusted Tourgen; yet, why would Tourgen remain an Elder if he knew the truth of Charis? What purpose could there be in remaining in a counsel of men that kept the followers of Marnin in bondage? Tourgen broke the awkward silent.

"You were the right choice. I watched you follow Marnin, and I knew you would never be content with Harness. Has Charis disappointed you? Is it all that I wrote to you about, my brother?"

"More." answered Bisbee hesitantly.

"And the Well? Did you make the great discovery?"

Mitch and Avonlea looked confused.

"Yes." Bisbee responded, trying to restrain his excitement.

"And now, to answer the question I know you have. I remained on the Counsel because Marnin loves the Elders. Most of them were simply misguided. They appeared confident, but they were searching for answers."

Tourgen paused, "Just like you were."

The Elder paused again, allowing Bisbee time to grasp his last statement.

"Bisbee, I was a part of a group of Elders who refused to ride the Beasts. We knew it was wrong to use the hideous creatures who were causing so much pain and suffering to our own advantage. Once I discovered the Well, my ignorance was replaced by truth. The desire to help my fellow Elders kept me in Harness. I knew I couldn't remain there forever, but I stayed until the rebellion in the hope of reaching some of them."

Bisbee looked over Tourgen's shoulder and noticed several of the former leaders of Harness in the group. How selfish he had been not to see their bondage.

"We have much to discuss my brother, but for now go spend time with your wife."

Mitch and Tourgen walked away as Avonlea rejoined Bisbee under the Willow Tree.

"I saw Lorelai walking down Ascending Hill. Is she still angry with me?" asked Bisbee.

"Yes. She spoke very little on our journey here. She's still resistant to this Land, but I think over time she'll come around."

"She has a lot of her mother's fight in her."

Avonlea smiled.

"Perhaps she does."

As they began to walk away, Bisbee looked back at the group.

"Who is that standing next to Lorelai?"

Avonlea smiled again.

"You mean the bearded man? That's Mitch's oldest, Merkel. Didn't recognize him with the excess shrubbery, did you?"

"Why are they holding hands? Do I need to go over there?"

"Leave them alone, Bisbee. They're in love. Some things have changed since you've been gone. Merkel's the only reason she came along."

Avonlea grabbed Bisbee's arm, forcing him to join her on their walk down to Living Stream.

"Bisbee, a muskrat just swam by. I think it smiled at me."

"He probably did. I'll tell you all about him."

Avonlea rested her head on Bisbee's shoulder. Leaning in close to each other, they shared a kiss that both wished would never end. Avonlea felt safe again, sitting close to the only man she had ever loved. His strength fed her soul. As the *stream flowed by, the red-breasted robin perched in the branches above, but all the pair could sense were each other.*

"Stephen's not in Charis, is he?" Avonlea finally asked.

"How did you know?"

"Your eyes, Bisbee, it's always your eyes that spill your secrets."

"He's in the Forest of Shedar. He's joined the Tribe of Gibbor."

The silence between them grew until it was deafening. Finally, Avonlea spoke in a soft tone that Bisbee could barely hear.

"I think it was the night he almost died. It changed him somehow. He blamed himself."

"He's determined to prove his worth to Marnin," Bisbee responded.

Avonlea signed wistfully, "Someday..."

A soft gentle breeze dried tears from two sets of eyes. They looked north toward Broken Dam as a flock of geese flew over the distant pastures. Bisbee spotted Marnin sitting on the dam. He glazed lovingly toward those who had chosen to follow him to the Land of Charis.

"Look Avonlea, it's him."

Like a spring bursting forth, fresh tears filled their eyes. Under the shade of the Willow Tree, sadness turned to joy.

Aliud est silvestri cacumine videre patriam pacis...et aliud tenere viam illuc ducentm.

ST. AUGUSTINE, *Confession*, VII, xxi

For it is one thing to see the land of peace from a wooded ridge...and another to tread the road that leads to it.

WORD MEANINGS

Harness- (Hebrew) 'raw-tham'- *to bind*

Magan- (Hebrew) 'maw-gaw'- *delivered*

Shedar- (Hebrew) 'shed-ar'- *endeavor, struggle*

Gibbor- (Hebrew) 'ghib-bore'- *strong, mighty*

Chayah- (Hebrew) 'khaw-yaw'- *to live*

Charis- (Greek) 'khar-ece'- *grace, kindness*

Marnin- (Hebrew)- *the one who creates joy*

Yabesh- (Hebrew)- *dry*

Naphash- (Hebrew)- *refresh*

Otser- (Hebrew)- *barren*

Karmel- (Hebrew)-*garden*

Adina- (Hebrew)- *gentle*

Tzaraath- (Hebrew)- *unclean*

The Journey North

1 Romans 6:2

2 John 8:32

3 Hebrews 4:12

4 Hebrews 5:14

5 Matthew 7:14

6 2 Corinthians 11:3

7 Galatians 2:20

8 John 21:1-3

9 John 21:12

10 C.B. Widmeyer, *Come and Dine* (library.timeless.org/music/Come…)

Ascending Hill

1 Matthew 16:24,25

2 Numbers 13:28,29

3 Numbers 13:17-20

4 Exodus 3:8

5 Numbers 13:3

Crossing Bridge

1 Evan Hopkins, *The Law of Liberty in the Spiritual Life* (Christian Literature Crusade), 45.

2 Romans 1:22,23

3 Romans 2:1

4 Romans 2:17

5 Ephesians 2:6

6 Ephesians 4:1

7 Ephesians 6:10

8 Galatians 5:2

9 Romans 7:13-20

10 Watchman Nee, *The Normal Christian Life* (Tyndale House Publishers), 166.

11 John 7:37

Hugabone

1 Galatians 6:12

2 Romans 6:1

3 Galatians 3:3

4 Romans 8:37

5 Galatians 2:19

6 2 Corinthians 3:7

7 Galatians 5:1

8 Galatians 6:13

9 Philippians 3:5,6

10 Acts 9:1

11 Philippians 3:8

12 Philippians 3:10

13 Galatians 6:12

14 Hebrews 12:2

The Beast

1 2 Peter 1:4

2 Romans 6:6

3 Romans 7:17

4 Romans 7:24

5 1 Corinthians 6:19,20

6 Jeremiah 17:9

7 Isaiah 64:6

8 Galatians 5:17

9 John 3:6

10 Oswald Chambers, *The Complete Works of Oswald Chambers* (Discovery House Publishers), 1107.

11 Romans 7:18

12 Romans 7:7-25

13 Genesis 3:11

14 Romans 8:7

The Magan

1 John 15:5

2 Galatians 2:20

3 2Corinthians 3:4,5

4 1 Corinthians 1:30

5 2 Corinthians 13:5

6 Hebrews 12:2

7 Romans 3:27

8 2 Corinthians 5:21

9 John 15:3

10 Matthew 11:28

11 Romans 8:37

12 2 Corinthians 5:21

13 Hebrews 4:9

14 Romans 7:15

15 Romans 7:24

16 John 15:5

The Mist

1 Joshua 6:20

2 Joshua 7:3

3 I Corinthians 8:1,2

4 Miles Stanford, *The Complete Green Letters* (Zondervan), 6,7.

5 Psalms 34:8

6 Galatians 5:1

7 Romans 10:17

Glassy Pond

1 Hebrews 11:36-40

2 2 Timothy 3:2

3 2 Timothy 4:3

4 John 7:4,5

5 Genesis 3:7

6 Genesis 3:8

7 Genesis 3:9

8 II Timothy 3:1-5

9 John Fox, *Foxes Book of Martyrs* (Fleming H. Revell Company), chapter 1.

10 Hebrew 11:38

Shallow Wells

1 John 5:39

2 Matthew 11:28

3 I Samuel 16:23

4 Edward Mote, William B. Bradbury, *The Solid Rock* (Hymns of the Faith; Tabernacle Publishing Company), 215.

5 Acts 2:42-47

6 Acts 2:1

7 Matthew 11:30

8 Psalms 1:3

The Forest of Shedar

1 2 Timothy 3:12

2 Ephesians 2:6

3 Ephesians 4:1

4 Ephesians 6:11

5 Ephesians 6:13

6 2 Corinthians 12:9

7 John 13:37

8 Colossians 1:27

9 Hebrews 12:2

10 Galatians 3:3

11 I Timothy 6:12

12 Exodus 14:13

13 Psalms 46:10

14 Romans 8:37

The Cave of Spit-Yak

1 Isaiah 53:6

2 Psalms 50:12

3 Genesis 1

4 Genesis 2:8

5 Genesis 2:21,22

6 Genesis 3:6

7 Genesis 3:8

8 Evan Hopkins, *The Law of Liberty in the Spiritual Life* (Christian Literature Crusade), 16.

9 Romans 7:24

10 Exodus 2:12

11 James 1:13

12 Romans 7:18

13 Romans 7:25

The Well of Chayah

1 John 1:14

2 John 1:29

3 I Peter 3:18

4 2 Corinthians 5:18,19

5 Acts 2:38

6 Romans 8:11

7 Romans 5:8

8 Romans 6:3

9 Romans 6:2

10 Romans 6:6

11 John 8:24

12 Romans 6:11

13 2 Corinthians 5:7

14 Galatians 3:27

15 Galatians 2:20

16 Romans 8:37

17 Romans 1:16

Printed in the United States
By Bookmasters